SILVERTON GOLD

JON HOVIS

Published by Casa de Snapdragon Publishing LLC
Albuquerque, NM

Library of Congress Cataloging-in-Publication Data

Hovis, Jon.
 Silverton gold / Jon Hovis.
   p. cm.
 ISBN 978-0-9845681-0-9 (pbk.)
 1. Private investigators--Fiction. 2. Colorado--History--1876-1950--Fiction. I. Title.
 PS3608.O895S55 2010
 813'.6--dc22

                    2010042556

Published by
Casa de Snapdragon Publishing LLC
12901 Bryce Avenue NE
Albuquerque, NM 87112
20101015
Printed in the United States of America

For Roger, my friend and fellow adventurer

PROLOGUE

San Juan Mountains, Colorado, 1873

The old man struggled to climb the steep mountainside. The talus covered slope kept sliding out from under his feet every few steps, hindering his progress. He wasn't used to this altitude and was gasping for breath. Even though he had been in the mountains his entire life, working in various mines from Colorado to California, the Rocky Mountains around Silverton were thousands of feet higher than even he was used to.

The kids called him Old Man Wagner, but he was still Cole to his few friends. He paused once again to try and catch his breath. At 48, he was old for a miner and too old for this type of work. This was likely to be his last chance to strike it rich.

He looked back down the slope to the tree line far below where he had left his two mules, Betsy One and Betsy Two. He named all his mules "Betsy" so he could remember their names. The two animals stood waiting patiently, content to be rid of the load they had been carrying all day.

Cole looked around at the grand scene beneath him. Arrastra Gulch was a long branch near the Animas River valley, a couple of miles north from the tent city of Silverton. He was far above the valley floor on the right fork of Arrastra Creek.

Several weeks earlier, Cole Wagner had been exploring the furthest reaches of the gulch when he happened to look behind him, and that's when he noticed it—veins of quartz running vertically up the mountainside. From down below it was hidden from sight by a rocky outcropping. He was certain that no one else had ever seen it.

Excitement rose within him as Cole studied the vein. He had been mining his entire life and knew what to look for. "This is going to be my lucky strike!" he told Betsy One whose only answer was a flick of her ear. Finally, after more than twenty years, he was the first to find a new lode, and hopefully a rich one.

Well, he reminded himself, *I'll have to get a sample first.*

Cole Wagner had always been a step behind in his career as a miner. Arriving in California in 1850 as a young man, he was a year late for the gold rush there, and by the time he had arrived most of the gold had been panned out of the best spots. He had been able to find some flakes while placer mining along a small creek, but finally had to go to work for someone else who had struck a lode higher up in the hills. Hard rock mining was back breaking work, and he had done it all. From drilling to blasting, mucking and even working in the smelter, Cole knew the mining business backwards and forwards and hated it, but how else was he going to get rich?

He had followed every gold rush when it was announced and like most, was a step behind the richest strike. He had tried his hand at silver mining when the Comstock Lode was discovered. But like most strikes, most of the valley had claims already staked by the time he had arrived. That meant the only work available was for someone else and that meant he was never able to get rich.

The only consolation he found, after years of studying the business, was that no one else was getting rich either. The mine owners spent their profits on improving the mine with new equipment and paying the miners—most of them ended up broke in the end when the mine played out. The miners themselves spent most of their pay whenever they got into town on gambling, whores, and, if there was anything leftover ... supplies.

No, the only folk who made any money in a mining town were the prostitutes, saloon owners, and shopkeepers ... and usually in that order. But Cole had a plan. When he found his lode, he would stake a claim, get the ore sample assessment and then sell the claim for enough money to live out his days in comfort and idleness with Betsy One or Two, he didn't know which yet, to keep him company.

Cole took another deep breath and looked up the slope toward the rock outcropping. He would set up his camp at the base of the vein and get to work, if he could just get there. When he had studied the hillside through his looking glass the week before, he had seen a game trail coming out of the trees where he had left the two mules. The trail went downhill, but he figured that it would get him close and then all he had to do was make a short, uphill climb across the talus. *Sure looked easier from down there, you fool*, he chided himself. It would have been easier to come in from the top, but there was no way of knowing that from down at the bottom. It was going to be difficult no matter what; the peak behind the vein was over thirteen thousand feet high- not something that he wanted to try and tackle.

As he hefted the pack back onto his shoulders, Cole wondered if he had brought enough supplies. He had figured on being out here for only a couple of days to get the ore sample that he would need, but it was taking a full day just to get to the site. He had left Silverton early in the morning with his supplies, and the journey had been all uphill. With Silverton at some nine thousand feet in altitude, it only got more difficult with each step. Now with a hundred pounds of tools and gear on his back, he thought he would never make it. *Well, I guess Betsy One and Two will have to keep each other company tonight,* he thought. *I ain't gonna make it back down there today.*

Cole took his pick axe out of the pack and used it to pound the ground in front of him as he took each step. Making a slight impression on the loose rock helped to keep him from slipping.

With his heart pounding and his lungs wheezing for more air, the old man slowly gained on his target. He was more than halfway up the slope now and he could see the base of the vein where it disappeared into the mountain. A cold breeze picked up, reminding Cole that winter was getting closer. He would have to get his sample quickly; once the snow started falling there would be no access to these high mountains until the following summer.

It was no wonder that this site had not yet been found. With the short summer season, there was little time to work a claim let alone scout the area and find it to begin with. Plus the Brunot Treaty had just been signed with the Ute Indians and Chief Ouray, legally opening up this area to exploration. There had been some activity in earlier years; the Baker party had first come in 1860 with little success, and then the War Between the States distracted folks for awhile. Finally, George Howard and some others came in 1871 for some prospecting and set up the town of Silverton at what had been called Baker's Park. Still, it had taken three more years before any permanent settlement was established. Now, Cole Wagner intended to be among the first to establish a profitable claim. There was no placer mining to be had which meant that all the gold was still in the mountains—the hills had not eroded enough to wash any of the gold into the valley streams. That meant hard rock mining would be king in these parts, hard work in which Cole had no intention of being a part. He would sell his claim to the highest bidder and be off to warmer and gentler environs to live out his days.

As he looked up while exhaling a huge gasp of air, Cole found himself within a dozen yards of his vein. He leaned back and gazed up at the streak of white quartz as it reached almost two hundred feet higher than where he stood. Finding a burst of energy, Cole scrambled up to the base of the vein and touched it for the first time. Feeling a chill run through his fingers, he stood there and smiled. "I'm gonna be a rich man," he told the rock.

With little time to lose, Cole started scrapping out some of the loose rock to make a flat surface on which he could work. He laid out all his tools; sledge hammer, several drills of different sizes and lengths, a long copper spoon, and some black powder which he placed off at a distance. Next, he made sure his food and water was secure in the pack and set it aside for later.

Cole stood at the base of the quartz vein and studied it for a few minutes. He would need to drill holes in several locations in order to blast out the ore. It would have to be done in just the correct locations and with just the right amount of explosive. Years of mining experience had brought him to this point, and he was going to do it right the first time.

Starting with a small drill, along the side of the vein, Cole started pounding the drill with a small hammer. Once the hole was started, he picked out a larger drill and the sledge hammer and really went to work. He would lay in several strokes with the hammer and then rotate the drill, keeping it from getting stuck. Every so often, he would pull out the drill and use the long copper spoon to remove the stone dust that was in the hole.

It took several hours of work, but eventually the hole was drilled. Cole worked well into the evening and by now he could barely see. He would have to quit for the night and finish the rest of the drilling the following day.

Old Man Wagner sat back against the rock and pulled out his food. After draining half of the canteen, he ate most of the loaf of bread and a small wedge of cheese. He was exhausted from the long day of hard work, but it was a good feeling of accomplishment. Too tired to bother cleaning the dust and sweat from his face and beard, and too tired to notice the millions of stars starting to dot the sky, Cole closed his eyes and fell into a deep, satisfied sleep.

Early the next morning, long before the sun could find its way above the mountaintop, Cole was back at work. The sound of steel pounding against the long rod of the drill was ringing down the slope so that even the mules could hear it. Betsy One and Two were stamping the ground, wanting to move from their confinement, but they would have to wait.

Cole worked throughout the morning, drilling seven holes in and around the vein. Each hole would get a charge of powder which would blast out at different times. Each explosion would be timed to blast the rock in a certain way so that it would crumble nicely right out of the cliff. The center hole would go first to create space, and then the side charges would go next, exploding everything in on itself. Finally, the top hole would go off and hopefully the quartz would drop right down in front of itself so he wouldn't have to chase it down the mountainside.

Cole carefully packed the powder into the holes, cut the fuses to the correct length and tied them all together. Next, he made sure that all his tools and supplies were safely out of the way. He took a deep breath and lit a match.

When the fuses took off, he calmly walked around behind the outcropping and waited for the explosions. Fifteen, twenty seconds ticked by and the first blast went off, quickly followed by the rest. Cole counted the explosions as best as he could and then waited a couple of minutes for the dust to settle. He could hardly contain himself. The time had come to see what was going to be inside the rock. He peered around the outcropping to spy the pile of ore littering the ground. It lay there just like he had planned, and it looked like all the charges had gone off. The last thing he needed at this point was to pick up a rock and have an unexploded charge go off in his face. He knew way too many miner friends who left this world early in that manner.

The old man's excitement was growing. This was the moment. His entire life had come to this point in time. He picked up a few small pieces of quartz and rock and studied it closely—something sparkled. Retrieving his sledge hammer, Cole broke open the quartz piece from the rock. As he turned it up towards the sun, there it was ... a whole streak of tiny particles, glistening in the late afternoon sun ... GOLD!

CHAPTER ONE

Chama, New Mexico, 1889

The three men sat on their horses, patiently waiting for the train to come by through a place called The Narrows. Their horses, ranch bred quarter horses, were well suited for the mountainous terrain and were well acclimatized to the area. The men sitting on them had stolen them two years earlier.

Edwin Jones looked at his two sons and liked what he saw — tough, street wise, and not afraid to face anything. Having spent most of his life behind bars, he had had little to do with their upbringing. His wife, Mary, had died of heartbreak after realizing much too late that her husband was just a common thief and cattle rustler. By that time his eldest son Ben was old enough to raise his two younger brothers after his father had been caught stealing horses from an army depot.

Edwin Jones had spent the last twelve years of his life in Fort Leavenworth Penitentiary, a military prison, breaking rocks for a living and planning what he was going to do when he got out.

Unlike his wife, his sons idolized their father. Slim, so called because he was tall and as skinny as a stick, was his middle son; not too bright, but he was good with things mechanical. His real name was George, but only his mother had called him that. Ben was sly and could think on his feet when needed, and he was fairly good with a six-shooter. The youngest, J.T., hard working and full of youthful enthusiasm, was not there today because he was up in Silverton working at the local post office.

It was all part of a grand plan that Edwin had been working on for several years. As he sat rotting in prison, Edwin kept up with things by reading the newspapers whenever he could get a copy off one of the guards. The mountainous areas west of Denver were booming with mining towns, and mining towns meant gold—and gold could be stolen. It certainly was a lot easier than digging it out of the ground for oneself.

Edwin had set his sons into motion preparing for the day he was to be released. J.T went to Silverton to find a place where he could watch for the gold shipments before they were sent out. Ben and Slim had found a secluded place along the railroad that they could use as a hideout, and they had discovered that Chama, in the territory of New Mexico, fit the bill. It was a perfect location, sparsely populated and close to the trail heading to Santa Fe. Best of all, it was right where the train started heading up to Cumbres Pass where it traveled real slowly. "Slow enough for someone to jump on board unnoticed," Ben had said. Even better was that they were stealing Colorado gold in New Mexico, making jurisdiction problems for the law. Edwin snickered, *well, that's their problem!*

Off in the distance, the men could hear the whistle from the approaching train. The four percent grade of the rail line was about the steepest a locomotive could handle. Most of the freight trains were split up in the Chama rail yards and pulled up to the pass using two, three, and sometimes even four locomotives. Passenger trains usually could make it with just one engine pulling, but it depended on the number of cars that made up the train. Either way, the trains traveled slowly going up the steep, winding grade.

The three outlaws waited along a gouge that had been cut through the rock, just wide enough for the tracks. The jump from the rock to the top of the train car would only be a couple of feet, and with a slight curve on the track, it was out of sight from anyone on the train or from the brakeman who might be looking along the length of the train.

Ben and Slim got down off their horses and gathered their gear. Edwin Jones took the reins of the other horses and moved off up the hill a ways, just to make sure no one saw him. He would wait until his sons made the jump successfully, then ride further up the tracks to the rendezvous point.

Excitement was growing among the men with the approach of the train. *Would this really work?* Ben asked himself. They had been planning this operation for months, years really, and now the moment was here. If they were successful, they could do this every time the train passed, provided it had the gold on board.

Ben checked himself. He had his trusty Colt at his side, a bag with several tools inside, and his hat pushed down low on his head. Slim calmly sat there, seemingly unimpressed with the entire operation, picking some dirt from under his fingernails. Ben nudged him, "Get ready!"

Slim looked back over his shoulder, "That train ain't even close yet, look how slow it's goin'."

"Well, at least get down off that rock so the engineer don't see ya!" Ben retorted.

Slim laughed and rolled down off the rock and watched his brother. All he had to do was wait for Ben to give the word and he would go. His brother always knew when and what to do. Slim didn't have a care in the world.

The late train out of Chama was a combination of empty freight cars and flat cars hauling logs. The time of day and the fact that it wasn't a passenger train meant that the combination baggage car and mail car was unoccupied. The early train heading west and the afternoon train heading east always pulled a mail car that had employees that worked in the car. As the train stopped at each settlement, the workers would set up shop, taking in mail from customers and handing out mail as required. When the train was in motion, the workers would sort the mail, getting everything ready for delivery. If there was no stop scheduled, then they would throw out the mail bag at the station and pick up the outgoing mail from a bag that hung from a pole at the end of the depot.

For Edwin Jones and his boys to steal the gold shipments without being caught, they had decided that they would hit the secure baggage car on the evening train. Railroad officials always made sure the door to the combination mail and baggage car was securely locked. They were confident that no one could break in and steal anything, especially the gold. It wasn't widely known at the time, but all the gold being shipped out of Silverton and heading to Denver, was simply put in the mail. Some fool had put it in a story in the Kansas City newspaper which Edwin just happened to read while he was in prison. That sent the wheels in motion with this wild scheme of his. Edwin figured that they could hit the train many times before anyone figured out how they were doing it, and they would make so much money that they could live out their days in luxury.

Ben watched the train chugging around the last bend just behind their position. There were two 2-8-0 Class 56 Baldwin's helping a 2-6-0 Mogul locomotive up the incline. Thick, black smoke billowed out of the smokestack of each engine as the fireman threw shovelfuls of coal into the firebox; each engineer kept the throttle just at the point of full power, ready to pull back just a touch if the wheels started to spin.

Behind each engine was a tender already half empty of coal, and then the baggage car was next in line. They would need to make the jump right away; if they missed, they would have to jump on a car further down the train and risk being seen by one of the brakemen or the conductor, plus it would take more time to get into the mail car.

As the locomotives chugged past, the two outlaws were almost choked by the smoke as they crouched next to the tracks. Ben struggled to keep the cinders out of his eyes as he watched for the baggage car. Suddenly, it was clear and time to jump. Ben slapped Slim on the leg and they both leaped down to the roof of the car. They landed at the same time, but Slim slid towards the edge of the car. Ben quickly spun around and grabbed his brother's hand and pulled him back up to the centerline of the roof. The two men stayed low as they struggled against the swaying of the train, crawling forward towards a small hatch.

This was to be the first test of the plan, to see if Slim could fit through the hatch. It was small and only used for ventilation for the mail car, but when they had looked at it before, it looked like it might be big enough for Slim to squeeze through.

The hatch was latched from inside, but it wasn't really a lock. Ben pulled a small pry bar from the bag and handed Slim a small pick. As he pried the hatch up a little, Slim slipped the pick through the space and was able to push over the latch. Ben pulled his gun, threw open the latch and quickly peered inside. It was empty, just like J.T. said it would be. Ben threw the bag inside and moved away so Slim could get inside.

Slim put his feet in first and shimmied his way down. He didn't wear a gun belt, which would get in the way, and his narrow hips went right through. When he lowered himself down to his shoulders, it was suddenly too tight. Slim looked to his brother for help. Ben quickly took his brothers hands and lifted him slightly while turning him at an angle to the hatch and then there was just enough room to wiggle through. The wood frame scraped his shoulders, but it wasn't too bad. Ben lowered his brother as far as he could and then let go. Slim fell just a couple of feet to the floor of the car and smiled up at Ben.

The lanky outlaw looked around the interior of the mail car, found a lantern, and lit it. With the interior illuminated, he could see to find his way around. One half of the car was taken up with baggage and large packages for the mail. The other half had a small desk, a safe, and rows of slots for sorting mail, and several mailbags hanging from racks.

Slim looked at the safe, he wanted to open it but he wasn't good enough to try that yet. Besides, the noise from the train made it very difficult to hear the tumblers in order to crack it. He simply made a note of the make so he could look into it later. No, they were here for something else. Bags of gold sponge— gold that had not been fully processed which was heading to a smelter in Denver. The bags were heavy, and they would only be able to take a few. However, it would still be a good payday.

Slim started sorting through the baggage, tossing aside anything that was too light or marked incorrectly. Then, back in the far corner, he found several smaller bags all tied together and held one up for Ben to see. "Open it up and check," his brother yelled. Ben had his head poking down through the hatch trying to see the lettering on the bag. The outer bag was a U.S. mailbag, but inside were several smaller sacks. Slim couldn't read very well so he hefted up the sack and showed it to his brother.

Old Man Mine was printed on the sack along with a list of contents and weights. "That's it!" Ben shouted. "Get as many as you can, and hurry!"

Slim cut off the rope that secured the bags together and pulled two of the bags over to the hatch. One by one, he lifted the sacks up to Ben who laid them neatly on the roof of the baggage car. When they had all that they could handle, Slim retrieved a length of rope from their bag and tossed it up to Ben. Using the rope, Slim pulled himself up until Ben could get a good grip and then the two of them heaved and twisted until Slim slipped up onto the roof.

They were just in time. The rendezvous point, Lobato, was just coming up. The train sometimes stopped in Lobato because there was a long siding for passing trains, and several cattle pens were there as well.

Ben pulled up the bag which was attached to the end of the rope and shoved the rope inside. The two outlaws then started tossing the bags of loot off the train and into the trees beside the tracks. When they were finished, the two climbed down to the platform at the end of the car and jumped off. They quickly scrambled into the woods and waited for the train to pass.

Two long whistles and one short blast from the lead locomotive signaled that the train was approaching Lobato siding. The train did not stop however, but continued on towards the trestle. The triple-headed train would stop there in order to cross the bridge - one locomotive at a time. The trestle couldn't handle the weight of three engines, so the train stopped here as well, as they unhooked the lead locomotive. The outlaws would have gotten off there if they couldn't make it off before reaching Lobato station, but the chance of being seen there was greater, and there was more of a risk of getting caught.

Back down the tracks, Ben and Slim were scooping up the sacks of gold as Edwin rode down with the horses. When he saw all the bags he gave out a whoop. "You boys did it!" he shouted gleefully. "Now let's get them loaded on the horses and get out of here before anyone comes along."

The two brothers had grins on their faces, proud to have succeeded and to have the praise of their father. They strung the sacks of gold, a pair on each horse, about as much weight as they could carry with a man riding, and rode off down the mountain.

After crossing the Chama River, they swung far to the west and then south, making sure to keep far from town. Ben had picked a remote location back there in the woods for their cabin, far from town so that no one knew where they lived. They even took a different route into town each time they went there in order to keep from making a trail. Even if someone knew the general location of the cabin, they were unlikely to find it.

Upon reaching the cabin, the three men whooped and hollered, and danced around with each other. They could hardly contain their joy. "We did it, boys!" their father exclaimed. "We did it!"

Edwin Jones pulled a bag of gold off his tired horse and opened it up. The gold sponge didn't look like much, it was still contaminated with other elements, but his eyes glazed over when he looked at it. *I'm finally going to be rich!* he thought.

Quickly sobering up, Edwin ordered his boys to hide the bags in the cabin while he made plans for selling the gold. It wouldn't get as much as pure gold of course, plus it was stolen, a fact that the buyers in Santa Fe would know and would use to their advantage. Still, he figured that they should get about ten thousand dollars for this day's work. Over the next few days they would get some supplies and a couple of mules to haul the heavy bags and prepare for the trip down to Santa Fe. The owners of the smelter there were always happy to have some gold, no matter where it came from, and they would in turn sell the refined gold to buyers from Mexico.

The Jones' gang would let things settle down for a few weeks and then they would do it again. Edwin would have Ben ride into Chama tomorrow and send a letter to J.T. in Silverton telling of their success and requesting info on the next big shipment ... they were going to do this again!

CHAPTER TWO

The trail to Santa Fe was hot and dusty. Even though they followed the Chama River south towards it's junction with the Rio Grande, the harsh desert was never far off the banks of the river. They occasionally rode into the Bosque to rest the horses and mules and to get out of the scorching sun for a while. The main trail was outside of the trees that lined the river.

Ben looked at his father, slightly slumped over in the saddle as he rode. "I still think we could have taken the train," he stated for the third time.

Edwin scowled at his son, "You know we couldn't risk getting caught with that gold! Besides, the Rio Grande doesn't run to Santa Fe, we would still have to hire a wagon. Now stop buggin' me about it."

Ben pulled his canteen and took another swig, nearly empting the container. He was certain that they could have brought the gold in a chest without anyone knowing what was in there, but he didn't want to risk saying anything more to his father. After years of prison and living on the run, his father was overly cautious and was going to stick to the old ways.

Ben tugged on the lead for the mules, trying to get them to step it up a bit. The miles were passing too slowly in this heat. He sure would be glad to get into town and enjoy city life for a bit. They would get a room for a few nights, enjoy the local entertainment, and get some decent food for a change.

Just as Ben was about to turn to his father to suggest they head over to the river for a refill, a group of rough looking men jumped out from behind some boulders that were at the foot of a small mesa. The men had been waiting here at a bend in the trail to ambush any travelers.

Ben instinctively went for his gun, but one bandit quickly levered a round into his Winchester, stopping Ben in his tracks.

"What do you want?" Ben asked.

The man with the rifle spat out some tobacco juice, wiped his mouth with a filthy sleeve, and laughed. "This is our land; you need to pay a toll to pass through."

Ben glanced back at his father who shook his head slightly. Edwin knew these men could do whatever they wished, they had the advantage with the rifle, plus there were four of them. He simply asked, "How much?"

The men smirked at each other thinking how easy this was. "Twenty dollars," the leader stated.

Edwin held out his hands in mock defeat, "Please," he implored them, "we are heading to Santa Fe to look for work; we have no money. Just five dollars to buy some food and a room." He held the money out for them to see.

One of the bandits pointed at the packs on the mules, "What's in those?"

Edwin pointed at the mules, "The packs? Those are my tools. I'm a carpenter."

The leader studied them for a moment as he scratched his scraggly beard, then he stepped forward and took the money from Edwin's hand. "I'll just take this. Next time you pass through here, you had better have twenty dollars or I'll take it out of your hide!" He spit again for emphasis, then the men turned and vanished just as quickly as they had appeared.

Ben took off his hat and wiped the sweat from his brow. "That was close," he whispered to his father.

Edwin just motioned down the trail, "Let's get going before they change their minds and search those bags."

They camped that evening near Chamita, next to a farmer's field by the river. The farmer was happy to let them stay when they paid for some food- a mix of beans, chile, and beef wrapped in a tortilla. It was the best food they had eaten in months. None of them could cook very well. Slim tried his best, he did better than his brother, but it was still lacking. Part of why they had left Slim at the cabin was that he was the acting homemaker, a job he didn't like, but Ben told him that that was his place.

Ben watched the water flow by as he thought about the events of the past few days. This scheme of theirs was going well so far, just a few more heists and they would be richer than they ever thought possible. The first thing he would do would be to hire a cook like the farmer's wife to make their meals every day. Then he would hire a maid to clean the house. Looking over at his father, Ben was going to ask him where they might live when this was all over, but his dad was already sound asleep. *Oh, well*, he thought. *It's been a long day; tomorrow we'll make it to Santa Fe.* Ben closed his eyes as a night heron flew by, looking for that first meal of the evening.

The following morning, in Denver, officials from the postal service were meeting with officials from the Denver and Rio Grande Railroad. It was not a pleasant meeting. Accusations and finger pointing were being thrown on both sides.

"How can several full bags of gold sponge just up and disappear?" the postmaster asked.

"The mail car door was locked when the train left and when it arrived, that theft is not our responsibility!" wailed the railroad official, "It must have been stolen or lost before it even made it on the train."

The postmaster waved an invoice in front of the man, "It was all signed for when it was loaded on the train."

The only man not fuming at the table was the owner of the Old Man Mine. Jackson Ives was actually enjoying the show in front of him. One party or the other was going to have to pay him for the lost gold. The shipments made through the mail were insured and he had the paperwork to prove it. "Well, gentlemen," he interrupted, "this arguing could go on forever, but I have other business to take care of. Just let me know when you get it all sorted out." And with that, Jackson Ives left the meeting leaving several men glaring at the door.

Later that day, close to suppertime, Edwin and Ben Jones made it to Santa Fe. They found the best hotel, a large two story adobe building with a restaurant and saloon conveniently just next door.

After making sure the gold was securely locked in their room, they enjoyed a large meal of steak and posole and then spent the rest of the evening in the saloon. Some discreet inquiries gave them a contact of a local man who operated a smelter as part of his blacksmith shop.

Early the next morning, the Jones gang took one small sack of gold and headed east out of the main square, looking for the blacksmith. They soon found a small courtyard with a carved wooden sign in English and Spanish leading to a workshop surrounded by corrals.

Anthony C'de Baca had lived just outside Santa Fe his entire life, just like his father and his father before him. He proudly told them that this rancho had been in his family long before New Mexico became a territory of the United States.

"But now, señors, I am a Nuevo Mexican, amigo to all. What can I do for you?"

Edwin tossed the sack of gold onto the bench. "We'd like to sell that."

The blacksmith opened the sack and examined the contents with a trained eye. Next, he turned and poured out the contents on a scale and weighed it while studying the mix of contaminants.

"Where did you get this?" he asked quietly.

"Does it matter?"

C'de Baca grinned at the men, "I suppose it does not," immediately knowing that it was stolen. "And you have more of these?" he asked.

"Yes, six total."

The blacksmith pretended to ponder the situation, "Gold sponge, contaminated, from an unknown source, six bags. ..."

Suddenly, he came up with a number, "Two thousand U.S. dollars, señors."

Edwin smiled, "You know it's worth a whole bunch more than that ... Twenty thousand."

The two bartered some more before finally reaching a price. It was just a little shy of the ten thousand that they wanted, but it was a good price and well worth the effort. They brought over the rest of the gold later that day and traded it for gold and silver coins and some paper currency.

That evening, the two outlaws lived the high life for a few hours, taking in a show, eating at the best place in the town plaza, and enjoying the rest of the evening in the saloon playing a few rounds of poker with several vaqueros.

The following day, they put half the money in a newly opened bank account in the local territorial bank and then packed for the trip back to Chama.

In Denver, the post office officials finally had to agree that they would have to pay the claim on the lost gold shipment. Jackson Ives happily took the check which he would deposit in the bank in Silverton, while the postmaster sent for an investigator to look into the matter. Losing that much money was not going to look very good to the officials back in Washington.

The two outlaws spent the first evening of their return trip back at the farmer's field. They could have traveled further without the load of gold, but they wanted to get another good meal from the farmer's wife, and a good place to camp along the river. Besides, as Edwin reminded his son, they had some business to take care of the following morning.

When they moved out the next day, Edwin took the mules and set out first. Ben rode out to the west of the small mesa where they had been ambushed on their way down.

After picking his way between sagebrush and cactus along the mesa top, he lead the horse to the edge of the mesa, Ben tied the animal to a piñon tree branch and then he crawled under the tree and peered out from below the thick branches. He could see the trail leading up the valley along the river just a hundred feet away, and his father riding up along the trail. If the bandits were hiding in the rocks below, he couldn't see them, but when they jumped out, he would be ready.

Sliding an old Sharp's rifle from behind him, he rested the gun in his outstretched hand and waited. The old gun was a relic from the war, but it still fired like it was new, and the range and power of the gun would knock a man clear out of his saddle at five hundred yards.

As his father drew nearer, Ben threw down the lever on the rifle which opened the breech, fed in a .50 caliber cartridge and pulled the lever home. He had seen a slight movement below him, and he just knew that the bandits were down there. Gently, he pulled back the hammer. ...

Edwin Jones pretended to ride along, half asleep, unaware of his surroundings. He had his hat pulled low, concealing the fact that his eyes were constantly scanning the rocks ahead of him, looking for trouble. He carried his pistol in his waistband, ready to pull at a moment's notice ... his hand barely an inch from the worn, wooden grip.

Just as he reached the base of the mesa, the bandits appeared as if from nowhere, the leader brandishing his Winchester. "Well, look who it is," he called to his companions, then he turned and pointed at his prey, "You had better have my money this time!"

Edwin just lifted his hat and glared at the bandit. That was the signal. A bullet tore through the man before he even knew what hit him, killing him instantly. As the thunder from the Sharp's reached them, Edwin pulled his .44 revolver and shot the next closest man. The bandit doubled over and dropped to the ground. Quickly, the other two men raised their hands in surrender.

"Which one of you has my five dollars?" he asked them.

They both pointed at their dead leader. Edwin motioned with his gun, "Well, get it out for me and empty out all his pockets, and yours too, while you're at it."

The men were afraid of this man with the cool, calm demeanor and they scrambled to fulfill his request. They pulled out every penny that they had on them and laid it at his feet.

"Now you see," he lectured them, "this is how you properly rob a person." With that he calmly shot each one of them in the heart. "Never leave a witness, and make sure you got it all the first time," he told the dead men.

When Ben made it back down off the mesa, he explored the base of the cliff, behind the rocks. "They've got a little cave back here," he told his father. "Besides some food stuff, there isn't anything in there."

"Must just hide out here during the day," his father concluded. "Well, let's put them in there." And with that, they dragged the bodies over and deposited them inside the cave.

The rest of the trip was uneventful as they made their way back to the cabin. Slim was glad to have his family back after a week alone. Ben told him all what had happened on the trip, while Slim tried counting all of the money sitting in front of him.

"Let's head into town and get a good meal," Edwin told his sons. "We also need to check and see if there is a letter from J.T.; it's time to do this again!"

CHAPTER THREE

Denver, Colorado, 1890.

Again, the meeting was not going well. The postal inspector, a man brought in from Washington just for this investigation, had just finished his briefing.

"You mean to tell me," the postmaster asked, "that after three missing shipments you still have no idea how the gold is going missing?"

The inspector shrugged his shoulders. "It simply disappears. The good news, however, is that there haven't been any thefts in the last three months."

"That's because there has been so much snow, the trains haven't been getting through!"

The official from the Denver and Rio Grande Railroad raised his hand, "If I may interrupt, gentlemen? I would like to suggest we get a private investigator in here to take over the case."

"Do you have someone in mind?" the postmaster asked.

"Yes. I have a friend who works at the Pinkerton National Detective Agency … I'll ask him to send his best investigator."

The postmaster looked around the table. No one objected so he turned back to the railroad man, "Do it. We can't afford to make another payout. Get him here as quickly as possible and find out who has been stealing that gold!"

At the cabin in Chama, the Jones gang was making plans. During the previous winter, Edwin had sent Slim to a guy he knew in Texas who was an expert in opening safes. Slim had been working diligently to learn the crafts of picking locks, which he found amazingly simple, and breaking into combination locks which took patience and considerable skill. After weeks of training and practice, he was getting the hang of it. There was just one catch though; there was no way he could break into a combination safe on a moving train. With the constant movement and noise, he wouldn't be able to feel or hear the lock mechanism.

Ben and Edwin had been discussing several options for trying to get into the safe on a moving train.

After several minutes of quiet thought, Ben asked his father, "Why don't we simply blow it? If there is enough pure gold in there, we only have to do it once."

"No, I want the option of being able to do it more than once. Besides, what if there isn't anything in the safe? We have to consider all of our choices."

Ben was studying the map of the railroad. "The longer freight trains are split up for the run up the steep mountain grade. That means that they sit up at Cumbres Pass until all of the train is put back together for the rest of the trip to Antonito."

Edwin liked where this was going, "Go on," he told his son.

"We jump on board just like we've been doing, wait until the train gets to Cumbres Pass, and then Slim cracks the safe."

"How long do the train cars sit waiting?"

"I don't know, maybe an hour?"

The two men looked at Slim, "Does that give you enough time, Slim?"

Slim rubbed his thin jaw while he thought about it. He wasn't good at figuring. "I guess so. Sometimes the train stops at Lobato and Cresco; I could get a head start on it at that point."

Ben wanted to make sure they considered everything. "What happens if he doesn't finish?"

"We'll have to have a backup plan. Perhaps we'll just forget it and jump off and try again later. Either way, we can't risk getting off the train at Cumbres since there are too many workers around who may see us. We need to head up there and find a good spot. There aren't as many trees on the downhill run to hide in."

"All right," Ben concluded, "Let's ride up there in a couple of weeks when the snow is cleared and take a look."

One week later, a slight, diminutive man, one inch and a hair under five feet tall, sporting a pencil thin mustache and a small trim beard, rode the train down from Denver, heading towards Silverton. Thaddaeus Ebenezer Smith was one of the best investigators that the Pinkerton National Detective Agency had. His unimpressive stature meant that most people ignored or dismissed him upon sight. He didn't appear as a threat to anyone - no matter whether they upheld the law or not. He found that he could pretty much go anywhere and do anything that he wanted without anyone questioning his motives; this made him a very effective detective.

As the train rolled along through the mountains heading towards New Mexico, he studied the terrain, his sharp mind already at work on this current case. Thad, as his friends called him, had studied the notes from the postal inspector, interviewed the postmaster and the railroad workers and was already working out a plan for his investigation.

Thaddaeus loved being a detective. He used his mind like an outlaw used a gun—as a weapon. Of course, he carried his own gun, a .32 Hopkins Allen top-break five shot revolver, in a shoulder holster under his left arm. The gun was small to match his small frame, and was difficult for anyone to know it was there, under his jacket, until it was too late. In his entire career, he had only killed one man. Most of the time, he either got the drop on his opponent or simply outsmarted them before any gunplay occurred. But it wasn't like he was unprepared. In his carpetbag, Thad carried several weapons, a .45 Colt, a Remington derringer, and a couple of knives. Several other tools of the trade were in there as well, a magnifying glass, a small telescope, and some small picks of different shapes and sizes.

Thad watched with interest as the train approached Chama. With trees, mountain peaks, streams, and wildlife to look at, he was really enjoying the train ride. He was planning to spend a few hours in Chama just looking around. With this small town being a major hub in the railroad operation, he needed to be familiar with the layout and workings of the rail yard and the town.

As the train pulled in next to the station, Thad gathered his bag and disembarked. He walked along the length of the train up towards the baggage car. *This is where they store the gold shipments*, he told himself as he inspected the car. It was sitting there, door wide open, but had several men working inside. *No way to steal it here*, he thought. The inspector was right about the thefts only occurring on the night trains. He looked at the door and the padlock which hung from the clasp. It was huge, and it was very unlikely that anyone could open it with the train in motion.

As he melted back into the crowd of people heading for the station, Thad made his way behind the building and up a short slope to the town of Chama. Sitting just above the tracks, Chama was a small town with the main street running along the rail line. Most of its buildings were on one side of the street. Thad spied a saloon, dance hall, and general store as he loitered on top of the rise. Behind the main stretch, there were a scattering of houses, a boarding house, and several corrals and a livery stable.

Turning back towards the rail yard, he watched as the passenger train pulled away, heading west out of town towards Durango. From there it would turn and continue north to Silverton, his final destination. After spending a few hours here, he would board the evening train to continue on his journey.

The activity at the yard seemed non-stop. There was an old rebuilt T-39 locomotive configured to a 0-6-0 wheel arraignment moving freight cars around, getting them ready for the mountain climb. A couple of 2-8-0 Baldwin's were pulling out of the roundhouse, hooking together to make up a double header train. Behind the roundhouse, a crew was working on an old 4-4-0 Baldwin, the workhorse of the west, probably to use it as a yard engine.

Further down the yard, rows of box cars sat, waiting to be used. A huge rotary snowplow engine rested after a busy winter season, and stock cars at the far end were being loaded from a corral for the eastbound train.

Thad felt that he had a good lay of the land, so he grabbed his bag and headed over to the saloon. A saloon was always a good source of information, especially in a small town where everyone knew each other.

Thaddaeus Smith strode confidently through the batwing doors of the saloon and quickly scanned his surroundings. A long bar stretched along one wall with a large mirror behind it.

There were shelves full of bottles. Even in the middle of the afternoon, there were quite a few men inside getting an early start on their drinking. A poker game was being played in one corner and a barmaid was watching them.

Several men looked up as Thad entered and one man laughed as he pointed at the newcomer, "Hey, no kids allowed!" The other men at the table laughed with him, but Thad simply tipped his derby hat and saddled up to the bar.

The bartender asked him what he wanted and Thad ordered a beer. He simply listened to the conversation around him for a while, stories about politics and trains were the main topics among the men.

After a while, Thad nudged the man standing next to him. "What do you think about the missing gold shipments?" he asked.

The stranger was only too happy to talk about the gold—it was much more exciting than politics. "It's a mystery," he began, "folks sure do want to find out what happened to it." He leaned down closer to his audience and whispered, "I think the mine never shipped it in order to get the insurance money."

"Is the mine in trouble?"

"Well, some think so, the Old Man Mine has had three new owners in the past three years. One month they are strikin' it rich, the next month they're broke and bankrupt. The current owner has stayed on for a while, though. Big money from eastern investors keeps him goin' I suspect."

Thad thought for a moment, "Has there been anyone around here who has gotten rich suddenly, or is spending money they didn't used to have?"

The man considered that. "Not that I've seen. Of course, there are always new folks coming through. Now wait!" he gestured suddenly, "That Slim fellow came in the other day and ordered a brand new suit for himself. That was strange."

"Why?" Thad asked.

"Well, he lives out in the woods somewhere, always looks out of place, being so tall and skinny. He ordered a tailor made suit so's it would fit him proper. That had a few tongues waggin'."

"Is there any law here in Chama?"

"No, not full time. We've got a jail for when folks get rowdy, but the marshal only comes up from Santa Fe if we need him."

"All right, thanks," Thad said as he turned around to leave.

The man watched him go as he suddenly wondered why all the questions. *That was also strange*, but he just shrugged and went back to his whisky.

Thad made a quick trip to the general store to ask the proprietor about this Slim character and anyone else who suddenly had changed their spending habits. He had to show the storekeeper his Pinkerton badge in order to get any information, but the man indicated that he wouldn't tell anyone about a detective snooping around. If the gold bandits were around here, he didn't want to spook them off.

"Do you know where Slim lives?" he asked the shopkeeper.

"No, no one knows. They keep to themselves."

"They?"

"Yep, there's three of them, I think, name of Jones. They come in for their mail every so often. They've been around for a couple of years and never bother anyone."

"Do you know where their mail comes from?" Thad asked.

"No, sir, couldn't say. It isn't marked with a return address, besides, mail is private and I'm not allowed to examine it."

"I understand," Thad replied. "Thanks for your help." He

quickly left the general store and walked back down to the train station. The late train to Durango should be in soon and he wanted to make sure that he was on it.

The 4-6-0 "Ten Wheeler" locomotive easily pulled the two passenger coaches and a baggage car through the low hills and mesas of southern Colorado. The ride was a pleasant one as it alternated between plains with yucca and sagebrush and juniper and piñon covered hills.

As they approached Durango, Thad got his first glimpse of the Animas River as it snaked its way down the valley. Shaded from the setting sun by high mountains to the west, it appeared wide and deep. Some glimmers of light indicated that there was some whitewater.

The train rode past the roundhouse and pulled in at the station. Thad got off the train with the other passengers as there was no night service to Silverton. He walked a block east of the station and gazed down the main street of the town. Durango appeared to be a brand new town, but, as one of the passengers had told him, it was due to the fact that just last year most of the town had burned to the ground. All the new buildings were made of brick and stone, and were built to last. Finding a large hotel on the corner, Thad walked in and reserved a room. Although he was eager to get to Silverton, he figured he should stay here for a day and look around.

Durango was another major hub in the Denver and Rio Grande rail line, providing a main point for freight, passengers, and most importantly, ore, to be shipped. Plus, there were coal mines nearby, which were very important to the railroad. The town had an impressive smelter, farming along the fertile valley, and a thriving cattle business. A large and growing western town, Durango would make a good place for someone stealing gold to hide out. Thad figured that he would talk to the town marshal the next day and sniff around a little bit. He really wanted to start his investigation in Silverton, but it made more sense to start asking questions in Durango since he was already here.

The next morning, awakened at sunrise by a blowing train whistle only a block away, Thad stretched out the kinks in his muscles and got dressed. He put on dark trousers, a gray waistcoat with a matching sack coat, and a floppy bow tie. Next, he put his revolver in his shoulder holster, checked his hair in the mirror above the washstand, and headed downstairs for breakfast.

Thad read the morning paper to see if there was any news and then headed out. The spring morning air was clear and cold, but the rising sun promised to make it a warm day. The town was already busy with folks setting up shop while others were heading to the train station where freight was being loaded for the east run.

Thad slowly strolled down Main Avenue and studied the layout. His mind was always working. If he was an outlaw, what would he do? Would he live here in Durango which was a bigger town and easier to blend into or was a smaller place like Chama better? He would have to mull over these questions in the next few days.

When he reached the jailhouse, he walked in and found Marshal Theodore Morton sitting … actually sleeping … at his desk with his feet propped up on the corner of the desk.

Marshal Morton was an older man who had watched the town grow up. Originally brought in by the railroad, he had served as marshal for over ten years and knew the area and the residents well. He spent years fighting Indians and fought in the

War Between the States and was respected by the town folk as being tough and wise.

Thad stepped forward and tapped the marshal on his boot. The next thing Thad knew, Marshal Morton opened his eyes and had his gun trained right at him!

"What can I do for ya, sonny?" he asked.

Thad opened his coat and slowly took out his Pinkerton's badge. "I'm Thaddaeus Ebenezer Smith, I. ..."

"That's quite a name for such a small man," the marshal interrupted.

"Well, sir, my dear mother, being of short stature herself, felt that a large name would be something to live up to. She was always disappointed in the name 'Smith', so she felt it necessary to make up for it with my other two names ... but you can call me 'Thad'."

Marshal Morton grinned and put down his gun. "So, Thad, you're here about the missing gold, huh?"

"Yes, can you tell me anything about it?"

"I can tell you it didn't happen here," Morton replied. "The local smelter has its own security force and they are really good. The gold is watched from the moment it arrives right up until it's loaded on the train. I personally watched the mail car all last season just to make sure nothing was happening here. Wherever that gold is going missing, it's either in Silverton or along the rails east of here. I can guarantee you that."

Thad was sure the marshal was sincere, but was he right? These thieves seemed to be bold, but discreet. In his opinion they could be anywhere. "All right, Marshal, I appreciate the information. I have to be on the noon train to Silverton, so I need to get going. Can I count on you if I find anything?"

Marshal Morton stood up, "Of course. Just send a telegram if you need to, or stop by anytime."

The two men shook hands and Thad made his exit. He had much to do today and he was eager to get going. After a quick visit to the hotel to collect his bag, Thad headed over to the train station and bought a ticket for the forty-five mile trip north into the San Juan Mountains and Silverton.

CHAPTER FOUR

Silverton, Colorado, 1890

J.T. Jones sat in the corner of the Grand Hotel while his boss, Postmaster J.M. Buzzard, was droning on about mail security. J.T. couldn't wait until his shift was over and he could go over to Blair Street and visit his favorite girl.

The post office had just been moved into the Grand Hotel since Buzzard owned it and J.T. had moved with it. Being able to read and write fairly well made him a good employee and his boss trusted him completely. J.T. smiled slightly at the thought. *If only he knew.* His only purpose here was to gather information on the gold shipments heading out. Since the local mines and smelters were trusting enough to ship their gold through the local mail, he had firsthand knowledge of when and where. It had only taken a short amount of time to know who the various employees were at the smelter. This gave him the opportunity to know when they were shipping out pure gold bars. And then when the milling and mining owners came in with bags of unrefined gold, all he had to do was check which train they left on and quickly send out a telegram to Chama.

The plan was working like a charm and with winter finally over and the trains running in the high country again, the shipments would start up again anytime ... and he was ready.

"J.T., are you listening to me?" Buzzard asked.

Snapping out of his trance, J.T. looked at his boss, "Yes sir, keep everything locked up."

"Right, we don't want any problems with theft like last year. Last thing I need is those inspectors bothering me again. We showed them that every shipment was signed for as it was being loaded. Wherever the problem is, it isn't here."

"Yes sir." J.T. repeated. He returned to sorting the morning mail as his boss walked away. *Actually, it does start right here. His* grin grew wider as he thought about it. *No one has any idea.*

Silverton sat in a valley at the junction of the Animas River and Mineral Creek. Surrounded by mountain peaks, it was a picturesque setting; the aspen trees were just beginning to leaf, their light green contrasting with the darker green of the pines. Higher up, there was still deep snow that wouldn't fully melt for another month.

Officially set up in 1874, the small town was chosen as the San Juan County seat and served as the main supply and destination for the area gold and silver mines.

After a spectacular train ride up along the Animas River valley, Thaddaeus watched with growing anticipation as they drew closer to the town. Many of his traveling companions had commented on the amazing feat of the railroad putting in these tracks where they had. Often, the line clung to a narrow shelf blasted out of the side of a vertical cliff, with a two hundred foot drop down to the bottom. The fact that it only took a year to build was even more amazing.

Thad had his head stuck out of the window of the coach as the train pulled into town so that he could study the layout of the town. With three blasts of the whistle, the train stopped at the station and everyone began to get off. Most folks were staying in Silverton, but there was a line being built by the Silverton Northern that headed up the valley, eventually to reach Animas Forks, for anyone who was continuing on.

After retrieving his bag, Thad stepped down from the coach and walked into Silverton. The town was laid out in a simple grid, with Blair, Greene, and Reese Streets heading north/south, and numbered streets running east/west.

Blair Street was the red light district—every other building was either a gambling or dance hall, saloon, or bordello. They each had rooms on the second floor for the girls, and between each large building was a small crib, usually containing four rooms for independent prostitutes. *It's easy to see what the main source of entertainment is around here,* Thad thought as he strolled along the street. There were even opium dens in a couple of places. *What a town!*

As he continued over to Greene Street, he could see that this was the main thoroughfare through town. There were hotels, shops, government offices, and other respectable businesses here. Greene Street seemed to be the dividing line between the different classes of society. Further west, homes and a church could be found, proving there was a respectable side to this town. Just north of the city hall there was a smelter.

Off in the distance, Thad could see a large mill for processing ore. The building was huge, even from this distance, and it was built on the side of the mountain. They used the hillside to their advantage, as the ore was fed into the machines from the top and was worked downward as each level pounded the ore into smaller and smaller fragments. The pounding of the stamps could be heard as the sound echoed down through the valley, drowning out the sound of the train as it pulled out of the station.

Well, time to get a room, he thought. Thad made his way to the Grand Hotel and checked in. As he was waiting in the lobby, he noticed that the post office was in the lobby. *That's convenient.*

Suddenly, the manager appeared at the counter and looked down at his customer, "Can I help you?"

"I'd like a room for a couple of weeks," Thad answered. "Also, I was wondering if you could tell me how to get to the Old Man mine?"

"Are you a miner?"

"Hardly," Thad replied with an air of snobbery, "I'm here to look at ore samples." That was to be his cover story as he worked to uncover the mystery of the stolen gold. Now that he was here in Silverton, he didn't want anyone to know who he was so as to keep from scaring off or warning the bandits.

"Well," the manager continued, "you could walk, hop the train or hire a horse. You already missed the train for today, but there'll be a couple tomorrow. But it's only a couple of miles ... you head up to Arrastra Gulch and then about another mile up the gulch. Can't miss it," he continued, "it's only the biggest operation up there, just follow the noise."

"Thanks," Thad said as he took his room key. "I'll head out there tomorrow." It was too late in the day to go there today and still have time to make it back before dark. Besides, there was plenty of snooping around that he could do here in town.

Thad spent the rest of the afternoon sitting in the hotel lobby, reading, or pretending to read the newspaper. In reality, he was watching the post office worker. J.T., as he learned was his name, seemed to be an efficient worker. He knew all his clients by name and usually had their mail in his hand before they even made it to his desk. Behind him, a small closet held larger packages and the mail bags for the evening train.

As the day drew to a close, J.T. closed and locked up his

desk, grabbed the mail bags and shouted a farewell to Mr. Buzzard. He ignored the insignificant man who had been sitting in the lobby for over an hour as he walked briskly through the building to the front door. J.T. was always in a hurry at this time of day; as soon as he was off of work, he could spend his evening with some drinks, maybe play some poker and then spend the night with his girl. There was always something happening and he was living large. He did not have time to notice the man who was discreetly following him.

Thad watched from a distance as the postal worker dropped off the mail bags at the station. The mail car was already on the main line, ready for the late run down to Durango. J.T. met with the porter who loaded the bags, signed the roster, and the two of them made sure the door to the railroad car was locked.

That's fairly straightforward, Thad thought as J.T. made his way down Blair Street. Finally off of work, the man wasted no time in heading to his favorite saloon.

The Alhambra Theater was a large building that housed a saloon, gambling tables, and a stage for shows. Since it was still early in the season, there wasn't a show tonight, but a singer was trying her best to entertain. Most of the men who had rolled in early were more interested in the poker tables.

J.T. quickly jumped into the action. He grabbed a beer from the bar and found a seat at a table. He wasn't a very good player, but that really wasn't the point. It was a way to let off steam and enjoy the company of others. Sometimes he won, and sometimes he lost. For the most part, he felt that he broke even, that is if you don't count buying drinks and buying ladies.

Thad slipped inside the front door of the establishment and found a seat in the corner. He sat quietly and watched his quarry. No one noticed or bothered him the entire time he was there, and that was just how he liked it. He watched as J.T. lost most of his money on this evening. The young man didn't even seem to mind. When he was just about out of cash, there was a commotion just outside. Men, curious about the noise, rushed out to see what was going on. Thad peered out of the window and saw a crowd gathering. A dog fight was being organized!

Two men faced each other, each with his prized fighter, one a bulldog, the other some crossbreed with a wolf. The two dogs were straining at their leashes, eager to get at each other. As more and more men gathered, bets were being placed and the action was about to begin.

Having kept an eye on J.T., Thad watched as he pulled yet more money out of his jacket pocket. *How did he have so much to spend each evening?*

Suddenly, the dogs were released. They sprang at each other in a flurry of growling and barred teeth. The wolf was faster and quickly sliced through an ear of the bulldog with its long, sharp canines. An old hand at fighting, the bulldog ignored the attack and waited for the wolf to strike again. This time the wolf came in low and tried for the bulldog's neck. The bulldog used its weight to push the wolf down and grabbed its neck with its powerful jaws. The wolf squealed in pain as it rolled over and tried to get away. This allowed the bulldog to adjust its grip and go for the soft neck of its opponent. The wolf pushed and pulled his opponent, trying to shake the other dog off and get a bite in, but the bulldog simply held its grip, growled, and shook the wolf until the other dog stopped moving. There was a cheer from half of the crowd as they realized they had won and money was grudgingly exchanged.

Thad noticed that J.T. had been a loser. After handing over his money, he headed off down the street as the crowd dispersed. Discreetly following, Thad watched him go into a crib several blocks away. This was exciting work, just the sort of thing that he enjoyed—sneaking around in the middle of the night, following his prey. Thad had a sense for the criminal mind and something didn't add up with this guy. *How was he able to afford losing a month's wages in one night?* This was one suspect that he would have to pay more attention to in the future.

After waiting for an hour, it became evident that J.T. was going to spend the night here. Thad gingerly stepped up to the front door and tried the latch. It gave under his hand so he carefully opened the door, trying to avoid having it squeak. As soon as there was enough space, he slipped inside and looked at the first door on the left. There was a name scribbled on the front, *Jewel*. He listened for a moment ... there was the sound of a man snoring, so he figured this was the girl J.T. was seeing.

Thad turned to leave and almost jumped out of his skin. Right next to him stood a woman, just a little taller than he. He had not heard her come up.

"Jewel is busy, how 'bout coming over to my place?" The prostitute was pretty, fairly young, and probably new at this game. She was wearing a low cut, red dress which showed off her slim figure.

Taking a moment to gather himself, Thad smiled up at the girl and stated, "Um, perhaps another time." He quickly turned and ran out of the door. He had never been approached before and it had rattled him.

Once outside, he took a few deep breaths of the cool night air and took stock of himself. He had stood up to outlaws, labor bosses, and politicians, all while keeping his wits about him. And all it took was one woman to rattle him. *I need a drink!* he figured, so he stepped over to the other side of the street and went into the Stone Saloon.

CHAPTER FIVE

Early the next morning, Thaddaeus Smith went over to the livery stable and rented a horse. It was a small Indian Paint which was well suited to its small rider, as well as the high mountain terrain.

Thad rode north out of town, past the smelter and up along the tracks which followed the Animas River. He could have taken the train, but it would have left too late, and he still would have had to walk all the way up to the mine. At this altitude it would have taken him hours.

Even at this early hour, as the sun had not yet topped the eastern mountain peaks, there were folks out beginning their day. Miners who had lost everything the evening before were walking to work, trying to beat the horn. Thad rode for two miles before reaching Arrastra Gulch.

Named for the ore crushing device used by earlier generations, Arrastra Gulch was a spectacular valley heading east off of the Animas. Sheer cliffs straddled the creek bed before opening up into a long narrow valley that ended in a bowl up by the distant mountains. The peaks on each side of the gulch topped out at over twelve thousand feet and were still covered with snow.

As he rode along, Thad passed a fork in the road which led off to the left and up to higher levels. He stayed down along the creek and followed the noise pounding down the valley from further up.

The Old Man Mill was the culprit; running twenty-four hours a day, seven days a week, the large stamp mill never ceased pounding the ore coming out of the mines. Getting closer, Thad could see large pipes carrying water to the mill from high atop the mountain. Using ever smaller pipes along the drop, the hydraulic power could be used for powering everything from the stamp mills to drills, and for washing the ore. It also provided water for the boilers that powered everything. Men were gathering at the mine entrance for the upcoming shift change. They were checking their lamps, gathering tools and supplies, and hitching mules up to ore carts. The previous shift would have spent hours drilling and blasting, and now it was the next shift's turn to muck out all the ore.

As the ore was brought to the surface, it was dumped down wooden chutes to feed directly into the mill. Other piles contained waste material and surplus that would be hauled out to various locations or kept until a slowdown in the mining.

As Thad sat there on his horse watching the activity before him, he was amazed at the operation. He had pictured a few small buildings and a hole or two in the side of the mountain, but this was different. It was almost like its own small city. Boarding houses for the miners, blacksmith shops, maintenance sheds and a dining hall were just some of the many buildings scattered here and there. Then there was the mountain. As far up as one could see, there were mine shafts at about three hundred foot increments, each one connected to the next by a tramway system. The tram was used for hauling ore down to the mill, and miners would ride the empty cars up to work. At the very top, there was a boarding house perched precariously on the edge of the mountainside. *Not someplace I'd like to sleep,* Thad thought. One gust of wind looked like it would take it down.

"Can you tell me where to find the owner or manager?" he asked a passing worker.

The man pointed to a building below the mill. "There should be someone who can help you in that office."

"Thanks," Thad replied as he tipped his hat. *Time to stop gawking, there's work to be done.*

He rode the paint down to the office and tied up the animal at the railing. Thad was gasping for breath by the time he reached the second floor of the stairs leading to the office. "If it's this bad down here, I wonder what it's like up there?" he pondered as he craned his neck to peer at the mountaintop.

"You get used to it, eventually."

Thad turned to find himself looking at Jackson Ives, owner of the Old Man Mine. "Mr. Ives, I recognize you from your description, I'm Thaddaeus Ebenezer Smith. This is quite the operation you have here."

"Thanks," Ives replied as the two shook hands. "I bought it after the previous owner went bankrupt. Along with several investors from New York, we got it for a steal. I put in that tram you see there and added almost a hundred workers. We've opened up several new shafts and upgraded the mill with new equipment. We now have twenty stamp mills operating day and night, and the new floatation separation is paying off big time. We are able to re-mill some older waste ore from those tailings over there and extract gold that was missed the first time around." Jackson looked at his surroundings with pride, "Yep, this is the best thing I ever did!"

"And the stolen gold?" Thad asked.

"Doesn't hurt me a bit. Everything that we ship out is insured by the post. And that gold is on the train when it leaves, so I'm not really sure why you are even here."

"I want to follow the gold from the moment it is milled all the way down the line. It's possible that whoever is involved works for you."

"I suppose you could be correct," Ives conceded. "Well, whatever you need, just let me know. I'll get one of my men to show you around. I believe you wanted to tell everyone that you are here to test samples?"

"Yes, we'll just say that I represent the investors, just keep it vague and no one should care too much."

"All right," Jackson agreed. "If it turns out to be one of my men, we'll hang him from the tram tower up there! Now, let me go find Gunther and he'll show you around."

Gunther Miller was the day shift foreman and had worked at the Old Man Mine for a dozen years. He had started at the bottom, mucking up ore, then worked as a driller before finally moving up to foreman. "Miners don't live long lives," he explained, "I want to be able to sit on the porch with my wife and grow old."

Thad laughed as they headed up to the tram house. He was already breathing hard trying to keep up with the foreman. Gunther scrambled up the tailing pile like a mountain goat and waited for his guest to catch up.

Pointing up the mountain, Gunther indicated the highest shaft opening. "That's where it all started, almost twenty years ago. Some old timer found this vein and struck it rich. But he was smart," the foreman explained, "he sold the claim for almost twenty thousand dollars and retired!"

"Does he live around here?" Thad asked.

"No, he was long gone by the time I arrived, but I'd sure like to find a strike like he did, but almost every inch of the San Juans has been scoured by now. There are mines all along the Animas, all the way up to Animas Forks, and up every gulch between here and there. No, I figure I'll work here for another few years and then head down to Durango or something."

The two men headed inside the tram building and watched as the ore cars swung around on the cable. Just as fast as the cars arrived, a worker dumped the ore down a shaft which led to the mill, and sent the car around to head back up the mountain.

"Hop in!" Gunther encouraged. "This is how we get up to the top." With that he stepped into an empty ore car and was quickly swept away. Thad watched the operator dump the next car, wondering how it would stay upright for the ride up, and timed it so he could jump in as the car swung by.

The ore car swung back and forth a few times and then settled in for the ride. Thad held on tight to the supports as he was swept up the mountain. The ride was exhilarating! At some points he was over fifty feet above the ground, watching with amazement at the scene below.

The car rattled over several tram towers before reaching the next level. He watched as Gunther jumped out at the top and he got ready to do the same. He counted down the seconds before the car arrived on the platform and leapt for safety.

"Whew, that was quite a ride!" Thad exclaimed as he wiped some perspiration from his brow.

"Good thing you made it, just last week a man fell out halfway up and died." And with that, Gunther turned and headed up towards the mine shaft. Then he turned and smiled, "Of course, he was drunk. ..."

Thad shook his head and followed the man up the stairs. They climbed up along a chute for the ore that was dumped out of the mine and down to the tram.

"This is three level, one is down there at the mill, but it's been closed. We weren't finding any more value in the ore samples; two level is just being used to move ore that is dumped from higher up out to the mill. Three, four, and five, that's the highest shaft, are producing the best grades right now. Come on," he gestured for Thad to follow him into the mine opening.

There were small tracks on the floor of the shaft for ore cars, duct work on the ceiling for ventilation, and even a string of electric lights. "We just put those in ... kind of nice, huh?"

There was also some piping on the floor. "What is that for?" Thad asked.

"Water," Gunther answered. "If we didn't pump it out, the shaft would flood. Water is always seeping in, and in some places it's pouring in. Step aside!"

They flattened themselves against the wall as a mule came along pulling several ore cars out towards the entrance.

Thad wondered in amazement at all the activity. The miner was covered in dirt and looked beat. Hauling rock all day- every day, at these extreme altitudes and conditions, and risking drowning or falling off the mountain, *this must be some kind of life*, he reasoned.

Gunther led him further back into the mine. In several places they had to walk around a hole in the floor, "These are vertical shafts which lead down to the lower levels," his guide explained. Thad was glad he had a guide or else he might find himself on a lower level by mistake.

Finally, after walking for what seemed like a mile, they reached the end of the shaft. There was a buzz of activity; workers were shoveling rock and ore into carts and ore cars. The rock had been blasted out from the vein on the previous shift.

Gunther pointed up towards a thin strip of white quartz running along the ceiling of the shaft. "That's the vein. We follow it wherever it leads us. The drillers poke holes along each side of the vein, the blasters load it with dynamite, and everyone runs for cover." He chuckled. "Not really. It's all very controlled. The blast is timed very carefully and there is only just enough powder to bring down the rock."

"Does anyone ever get killed?"

"Oh, sure. We lose a man almost every month. Either from a blasting cap accident or someone falls down somewhere."

"Incredible."

"Yep. Let's go this way and I'll show you around the mill." With that they stepped into a cross shaft and walked for awhile before finding a shaft that headed down to two level.

The mill was even louder inside than out. With each level, the ore was crushed to a finer and finer powder before finally being washed to separate out the gold.

The top level used giant rollers to break up the large pieces which then were fed down to the stamps. A cam system lifted each stamp and then let it drop, pulverizing the ore and causing a lot of noise. By the time the ore reached the lowest level, it was the consistency of fine sand.

From there, the ore was run across a sheet of copper impregnated with mercury. The gold would stick to the mercury and everything else would be washed away and dumped outside or further processed for the other metals that it contained.

Gunther had to shout directly into Thad's ear to explain, "Once a week they scrap the mercury off the sheet and retort the mercury." He gestured for Thad to follow him into the next room. Inside was a device that looked somewhat like a still.

"We heat the mercury until it is vaporized, it condenses in these coils and can be re-used, and the gold is left here in the bottom."

"Where do you store the gold?" Thad shouted his question.

"It's kept right here in this room, under armed guard, until we ship it out."

Gunther led Thad outside to where it was less noisy. He gestured around, "And that's it."

"Tell me about the guard."

"Tiny? He's worked here forever, even longer than me. I'll introduce you in a bit."

"And where do you ship the gold when it leaves the mill?"

"Well it depends," Gunther began, "That gold still isn't pure; it has to be refined one more time. So it depends on where we can send it. Usually we send it to the smelter in Silverton and then when they are done with it, it goes to Denver. Otherwise, we ship it to the smelter in Durango. We used to ship some of it all the way to Denver, but there is enough capacity here that we do it locally now."

"And you keep it guarded the entire way?"

"Yep, nobody messes with Tiny, as you'll see. But once the smelter gets it, it is out of our hands. Come on, I'll introduce you."

They headed down to the boarding house on the valley floor to find the guard. When they walked in, Thad knew immediately who "Tiny" was. He was the biggest man he had ever seen; he must have been seven feet tall and four hundred pounds!

"Tiny," Gunther prompted, "this man wants to know how you keep the gold safe."

Tiny rose from his chair where he had been playing cards and stretched his enormous frame until his head almost brushed the ceiling. Without saying a word, he walked over to his bunk and picked up his gear. His gun belt held two .44 Remington revolvers, and a string of ammunition, and he hefted up a ten gauge double barrel shotgun along with a bandolier of shells.

Gunther turned to smile back at Thad, "Only one man tried to steal a gold shipment," he turned back to Tiny.   "What happened to him, Tiny?"

"Dead." was the simple answer.

"Yep, nobody messes with Tiny," Gunther concluded.

"I can see that, thank you gentlemen."

With that, the two men headed back outside.   "Is there anything else you wanted to see?" Gunther asked.

"No, I think that covers it, thank you for your time."

Thad shook the foreman's hand and headed back to the office to collect his horse.

As Thad rode down the gulch back towards Silverton, he mulled over what he had seen and learned today. The operation at the mine seemed secure, and the employees who handled the gold seemed trustworthy and loyal. Plus, being isolated at the mine for months at a time, it was unlikely that anyone here was responsible for the thefts or supplying information to the thieves.

Thad was still highly suspicious of the post office worker, J.T., he had way to much cash on hand, especially if he lost it on other nights like he had the previous evening. His position was ideal for knowing when the shipments were going out. It was time to give him a second look.

CHAPTER SIX

Thaddaeus Smith rose early the next morning, ready to continue his investigation. He slicked back his hair, trimmed his short beard and checked his reflection in the mirror. Satisfied that all was in order, he donned his derby hat, checked his gun and headed out the door.

Silverton was just starting to stir at this early hour. Greene Street businesses had not opened yet and the town was quiet. Blair Street, which didn't shut down until well after two in the morning, was still sleeping in. Just one or two miners who had stayed too long were running back up the valley to try and get to work before they were late.

Thad wanted to get an early start and learn as much as he could on this day. It was Saturday and most businesses would be shut down tomorrow for church ... well, *at least the respectable side of town*, he thought.

Strolling down Blair Street, Thad found the little four-room crib where Jewel had a room. He quietly stepped inside and tried listening at the door again. Hoping to avoid an encounter with that other girl again, that girl he couldn't seem to get out of his mind, Thaddaeus made sure to be aware of his surroundings this time.

All was quiet in the room. He thought he could hear the gentle breathing of someone asleep, so he gently tried the door.

With a slight squeak, the door opened and Thad peered inside. Sure enough, J.T. was sound asleep next to a lady of the night. The room was sparsely furnished, just a potbelly stove, bed, small dresser, and a table that sported a red shaded lamp, in front of the window.

Thad took one more quick look at the sleeping figures and backed quietly out into the hallway. With a backwards glance, making sure that he was still alone, the detective left the crib.

Back in the street, Thad took a deep breath of the cool morning air, glad to be out of that place ... *unmolested*, he thought. It was still quiet out on Blair Street, but the rest of the town was beginning to stir. Thad decided to grab a quick bite and then head over to the smelter and see the operation there.

The Greene & Co. Smelter had been one of the first businesses built in Silverton and was owned by George Greene, one of the founders of the town. Located just north of the town, near Cement Creek, it had been dutifully serving the needs of the area mines for years, although it couldn't keep up with demand, especially during the short, busy summer months.

The building was long with a center smokestack that belched smoke non-stop. The ovens used to purify the gold sponge were kept running all day, every day.

Thad walked into the office and found the manager, J.A. Porter behind his desk, sorting through some papers. The older, balding man looked up at the newcomer, "What can I do for you?"

Deciding to stick to his cover story, Thad announced, "I'm working with the Old Man Mine, checking out some of their samples. I was wondering if I could get a tour of your smelter and observe your refining process."

Although Porter was usually a suspicious man by nature, he saw nothing threatening in the small man standing before him. "Sure, just give me a minute. The morning shift is just getting started."

Thad waited patiently until the manager finished with his morning counts. Porter filed away the papers and then stood up. "All right Mister, uh, what was your name?"

"Thaddaeus Ebenezer Smith," Thad stated proudly.

"Oh, right. So, what would you like to see first?"

"I understand that the gold is brought in under armed guard? Where do you keep it?"

Porter led him down to the end of the building, "We have a secure room right here with an armed guard present at all times. The gold, in whatever form, is weighed and recorded, and then stored until we can get to it. Each shipment is refined in one batch so we can keep track of it. Every mine produces different grades of ore, and even the same mine can produce different samples, depending on the location. So each batch is kept separate."

Thad felt that that was fairly straightforward, he was just pretending to be interested in the entire operation. "Can you show me the ovens?"

Porter led him to the center building which housed the ovens. "Depending on how we receive it, the gold is still contaminated with other metals. Here we superheat the metal and pour out the pure gold. From there, we can take the waste and separate out the silver, lead, tin and whatever else may be in there."

Thad felt his face burning from the heat generated by the red hot ovens, even though they were not that close. "What do you do with the refined gold?"

Porter led him to the other end of the building. "This is

another secure room. We weigh and record the final product and prepare it to be shipped." He handed Thad some papers, "This is the batch we shipped yesterday for the Sunnyside Mine."

The report showed the different percentages of various metals produced from the ore. It showed two fifty pound bars of gold were sent out. "You shipped this yesterday?"

"That's right; we try not to keep any significant amounts here for security purposes. Plus, the mine owners don't get paid until it is delivered to Denver."

Thad was starting to lose his temper, but he held it under control. He had been told that no shipments would be sent without his knowledge. The smelter obviously didn't get that message. "And you take it under guard to the train?" he asked.

J.A. Porter suddenly became suspicious, "That's privileged information, I can't share that with you."

"I understand," Thad replied, backing off, "I look forward to seeing the report from the Old Man Mine.

Thad quickly left the smelter and headed straight for the telegraph office, hoping that he wasn't too late. They must not have notified him of the shipment yesterday since it was from a different mine. He would have to make sure that everyone understood that he needed to know about every shipment from now on.

The Jones boys sat on their rock, waiting for the train. It was getting dark; the sun had already dipped below the western mountain peaks, casting long shadows across the slope. They would have just enough light to see what they were doing when the train arrived.

Slim was fiddling with some of his new tools—tools to help him open the safe, when Ben nudged him with his foot. "Time to get ready. Put that stuff in the bag." Slim stowed his supplies and crouched down behind the rock, ready to jump.

Just around the bend, a single locomotive was chugging up the grade. It was an evening passenger train and only had the baggage car and two coaches, not the best situation. They would have to work fast as the train would only be stopping for water up at the pass.

Ben looked over at his father just before the train arrived. Edwin Jones had grabbed the reins of the other two horses and was making his way up the hill, heading towards Lobato siding.

A cloud of smoke engulfed the two as the Baldwin locomotive passed by. Ben grabbed his brother and the two jumped from the rock. They had done this several times now and they landed with ease and quickly scrambled up to the hatch on the roof of the rail car.

With practiced precision, they opened the hatch, Slim slipped inside, and Ben passed down the tools. Once inside, Slim lit the lantern and got to work. The safe, standing proudly in the center of the baggage car, was a Corliss bank safe. One of the largest made. It was too heavy to move without a gang of men—and a hoist. Most outlaws would simply choose to blast the door open, but that meant only one shot at it, and you had to make a quick getaway. The Jones gang wanted to be able to open this safe many times and help themselves to the contents.

Slim set out his tools in front of the safe as Ben watched, his head sticking through the hatch. The safe had a large combination tumbler, most likely three or four numbers, and a key lock as well.

As his first order of business, Slim noted the position of the dial. His mentor had taught him that some folks forget to spin the dial after opening a safe, so the number currently showing may be the last digit. Next, he gently turned the dial getting a feel for it, trying to detect if there were any changes in resistance, indicating a possible location for the tumblers. After that, he simply sat down to wait. With the motion and noise of the train, he wouldn't be able to do anything else at this point.

In Silverton, Thaddaeus was sitting in the hotel lobby planning his next move. He most likely would not get anything done on Sunday with most businesses closed. Even though the mines, mills, and smelters all continued running seven days a week, there would not be any shipments. Perhaps he could take a day off. Just then, the girl from the crib jumped into his mind. With her long blond hair and slim figure, he found himself imagining them walking along the creek together. …

Thad shook his head to clear his mind. *Keep your mind on the job*, he admonished himself. He would continue tracking the post office employee and see what he did on his day off, but since he seemed to sleep in most mornings, Thad figured he would attend the church on the other side of town in the morning. *I wonder what her name is*, he asked himself. *I suppose it wouldn't hurt to head over there and find out; after all, I am a detective.* He stood up to leave, *but what does this have to do with the job?* Thad stood on the front walk debating with himself about what to do. Finally, he reasoned that she might know something about the case. *That makes it job related!* With a determined step, he walked over to Blair Street, trying to quell the fear creeping up in his belly. He was actually going to talk to her!

The late train to Antonito didn't make any stops until it reached Cumbres Pass to take on water. Ben was getting nervous—they might not have enough time!

As soon as the train stopped, Slim went to work. He put a long funnel next to the dial on the safe and slowly started turning. With half closed eyes, he listened intently as his fingers moved the combination lock with a delicate touch. Several minutes ticked by as he turned the dial back and forth, seemingly without making any progress.

Suddenly, the train car made a thump as the locomotive prepared to pull away. Slim's eyes opened wide as he realized he was just about out of time. With a flash, he turned the dial three times and landed on the number he had noted earlier. As the train pulled away from the water tower, he reached over and turned the latch ... it moved! All he needed to do now was pick the key lock and it was his. Turning to look up at Ben, he smiled his easygoing smile and then went back to work. Ben pulled his handkerchief and wiped away the sweat from his face. He was getting excited, *this is going to work!*

After choosing two small picks, Slim worked on the lock. Nothing precision here, he could do this while the train was in motion. A minute later he had the lock turned and then he opened the safe. Sitting inside the safe, on a low shelf, sat a heavy lockbox made of wood with metal bands. Slim turned and grinned up at Ben again who was gesturing for him to hurry. The train was gaining speed on the downhill run and they needed to get off as soon as possible.

Slim closed the safe and spun the dial and then gathered up his tools. Using the rope, Ben hefted the box which just barely fit through the hatch, up to the roof of the car, then the tools, and finally, his brother.

Outside, it was almost pitch dark—just a sliver of moon

offered some light to see. The two outlaws slid down to the edge of the roof and climbed down to the platform at the end of the first passenger coach. The train was passing through a field while going around Tanglefoot Curve which seemed clear of any trees or rocks so they tossed their bags out and made the jump. Ben landed first and rolled to a stop, seemingly unharmed. Slim landed a few feet away and smashed his face into the ground. Bloodied and embarrassed, he was otherwise okay. The two sat there for a while and calmed their nerves before heading out. It was unlikely that their father would be able to find them out here in the dark, so they would have to walk back up to their rendezvous point on the other side of Cumbres Pass. It was going to be a long walk, and a long night.

Thaddaeus Ebenezer Smith was stuck outside of the door to the girl's crib. Not physically, but mentally he was unable to move. His hands were sweating so much that he didn't think he could open the door even if he could will himself to do so.

Suddenly, just behind him, a shot rang out and a whole lot of commotion, as well as men, came pouring out of the Bon Ton Bordello across the street. Glad for the distraction, Thad stepped into the street to see what was happening.

Just then, a man, half dressed and trying to hold up his drawers as he ran, was high-tailing it out of the front door as one of the prostitutes ran out just a few steps behind. The woman, upset at something or another, raised her pistol to fire again at the fleeing man. Several bystanders tackled the woman before she could shoot a third time.

As things settled down, the night watchman rushed over to take the girl into custody. She was still in a huff over the incident and was trying to bite the officer's hand as he led her away to the jail. Thad was standing there in amazement as the crowd dispersed and made their way back inside.

"That's the second man she tried to kill," a soft voice said next to him.

Thad turned to find the girl in the red dress standing behind him. She smiled at him and waited for a moment before deciding that Thad was tongue tied. "Do you want to come in?"

"Uh, I, um … sure," he stammered, "but not for that, I just want to talk."

The girl smiled again, "Whatever you want. It'll cost the same." Usually they changed their mind once inside.

Ben and Slim were breathing hard. They had gathered their gear and made out for the rendezvous with their father at Cumbres Pass. It was all uphill and they had the heavy lockbox to carry as well.

"Next time, let's plan on meeting Pa further down the tracks," Slim suggested through labored breaths of air.

Ben stopped and looked back at his brother. "Do you think you can open this thing?"

"Sure, but why not just shoot off the lock?"

"It'll make too much noise, someone may come to investigate."

"Oh, yeah, I didn't think of that." Slim studied the lock as best he could in the darkness and then pulled out a thick pick and a long thin tube. After working for a couple of minutes the lock turned. "Got it!" he exclaimed.

They opened the lid of the box and looked inside. "That's it?" Slim asked.

Two bars of gold were all that were in the box, along with some papers.

"That's okay," Ben said, "that's almost twenty thousand dollars right there."

"Really?" Slim asked, "I guess that's all right then."

"Come on, let's get moving," Ben urged. "We'll hide the box behind those rocks and just take the gold bars."

They continued hiking up the mountain wishing like crazy that they had some horses; it was going to take several hours to make it up to where their father would be waiting for them, just west of the rail yard.

Thad was sitting on the edge of the bed, nervously fiddling with his fingers. Pearl reached over and put her hand on top of his. "So, what do you want to talk about?" she asked sweetly.

Looking into her pale blue eyes, thinking to himself how pretty she was, Thad tried to decide if he could trust her. Should he tell her who he really was and what he was doing here? "I, um, saw you the other night and I wanted to ask your name."

"And you saw it on my door. So, what is your name?"

Thad answered with his full, proud name.

"That's a wonderful name," she announced. "It comes from the Bible, right?"

He nodded his head while thinking that this girl was okay.

"Now, tell me more about yourself," she encouraged.

"Well," he began, deciding to trust her, "I am a Pinkerton Detective." Thad took out his badge and showed it to her.

Pearl jumped up off the bed and exclaimed, "You're here to arrest me? I paid my fine this month!"

"No, no," he held out his hands to try and calm her down. "I'm working on a case ... but what do you mean about a fine?"

Pearl sat back down and composed herself, "Prostitution is illegal here in Silverton. Each month we all go to the courthouse and pay a fine. That's what keeps the local government running, didn't you know that?"

Thad continued to be amazed, "I had no idea."

"Yeah," she went on, "the town doesn't have to charge any taxes because of what they collect from us girls on the line." She smiled, "I guess they pay their taxes through us!" She gave a little giggle at her joke.

Thad grinned with her and then asked, "So how did you get to be here?"

"Oh, my husband died in a mining accident and I had nowhere else to go. We had just gotten married too!" she looked suddenly sad.

Thad wanted to put his arms around her, but he was too bashful. "I'm sorry about that." He did manage to reach out and put a hand on her arm as they sat silently for several minutes.

After a while she looked at the man sitting next to her, "Tell me about the case you're working on."

Thad's mind quickly changed back to investigator. "What can you tell me about the girl across the hall?"

"Jewel? She has worked here for several years, much longer than me. She used to work out of the Diamond Belle, but now she works for herself. Jewel owns this crib; I have to pay her some of my share."

"And the man who stays with her each night?"

"I don't know much about him. I'm usually working when he shows up. I guess he's her boyfriend, but he still has to pay her double to spend the night."

"Does Jewel ever talk about the stolen gold from the trains?"

"Is that what this is about?" Pearl whispered.

"Yes, but you have to promise me to keep quiet about it. I don't want anyone to know that I'm here." Thad explained to her about his cover.

"I won't tell anyone," she promised, excited to have a secret. "Us girls are good at keeping secrets—why half our clients come from the 'respectable' part of town!" she giggled again.

Thaddaeus laughed with her while he thought about his next move as he checked his pocket watch, "I guess I should be going now, it's getting late."

She pretended to pout a little, "I guess you really did just want to talk, huh? When will I see you again?"

"You could come to church with me in the morning," he prompted.

"Church?" Pearl laughed out loud. "I can't go to that side of town," she explained, "we aren't allowed to go any further than this side of Greene Street. Besides, the churchgoers would run me out if I stepped foot in there."

"Well, perhaps I'll stop by afterwards."

"Just to talk again?" she teased. "It'll still cost you two dollars."

I'd gladly pay more, he thought, but he just grinned at her and made for the door. "Let me know if you hear anything." And with that he slipped silently out and crept past the other door and out the front.

Pearl watched him go through the crack of the door thinking that she liked the small, intelligent man. *No one had ever come just to talk before.*

By three in the morning, Ben and Slim made it to the pass. All of the railroad workers had gone to bed after the late train had passed and the two outlaws were able to easily slip past in the dark. They followed the snow shed down to the end of the siding. Just beyond that, there was a small lake where Edwin was waiting.

They plodded up to the small campfire and collapsed to the ground, too exhausted to talk. Ben simply took a bar of gold out of his coat pocket and handed it across the fire to his father and Slim did the same. Edwin held the two bars in his hands and watched the firelight dance off the gold. With sparkles in his eyes, he grinned at his boys. "You did it," he said simply.

"We did it," Ben answered.

CHAPTER SEVEN

Sunday morning found Thaddaeus Smith on his way to church. The Congregational Church on the west side of town held services each week for the "respectable" folks in Silverton. Anyone from Blair Street was strictly forbidden to attend, and most miners were required to work seven days a week. Occasionally, a miner would go stir-crazy after working for weeks at a time and would be allowed to come to town to blow off some steam. Once all their money was lost at the saloons, they would come to church if sober enough.

Thaddaeus walked up to the front step and waited as several families, dressed in their finest clothes, headed inside and then he followed.

The small building was packed with churchgoers so there was only standing room left at the back of the room. Thad found a support beam to lean on as the service began. A hymn, *A Mighty Fortress Is Our God* was sung, the voices loudly belting out the stanzas. Happily joining in, Thad knew the song from the Lutheran Church he attended back in Chicago. Despite the lack of any hymnals, the congregation knew and sang all the harmonies which lifted his spirits and made for a moving experience—it must have been heard three blocks away!

After a time of prayer, the preacher got up to deliver the sermon. Thad listened intently as a passage in the Gospel of

John, chapter six, was read about Jesus feeding the multitudes. Following the short message, Thad was encouraged by the closing verse.

And Jesus said unto them,
I am the bread of life:
he that cometh to me shall never hunger;
and he that believeth on me shall never thirst.

Thinking that the service would now be over, Thad soon realized his mistake. The preacher suddenly moved into an entirely new direction with the sermon and started preaching against all the evils of drinking, prostitution, opium, and fighting … basically life as he knew it on Blair Street. Thad glanced around the room wondering how many of these men had been doing those very things the night before.

After a few minutes, Thad started to tune out the preacher and allowed his mind to wander. He started thinking about Pearl and how much he enjoyed talking with her. He couldn't wait for the service to be over so he could run over to see her. *I wonder if she'll go for a walk with me*, he thought. Then he remembered that he had a job to do as well, *Perhaps I can do both at the same time.*

A loud thump from the pulpit jolted him out of his daydream. The preacher had just made an important point which he emphasized with his fist, to which several men added their "amen" and suddenly the sermon was over. They all rose to sing another hymn and then the service was over. Thad exited the building after shaking the preacher's hand and headed back to his hotel room to change, humming the melody to *Amazing Grace.*

In the small cabin near Chama, Ben was arguing with his father. The two were once again disagreeing on what to do and how to deal with the gold. "Let's just take one bar to Santa Fe and keep the other!" he challenged.

"It's stolen," Edwin retorted. "We have to get rid of it and get the money for it."

"But we can get more for it once we leave for California. I can take the train. ..."

Suddenly, Edwin exploded with rage and pulled his revolver with lighting speed and pointed it at Ben. "I told you not to mention that train!"

Ben's eyes grew wide at the outburst—he had never seen his father react in such a way. He just stood there, frozen in place, unsure of what to do.

Sitting at the table, Slim's eyes were also wide open, as well as his mouth. He thought for sure that Ben was going to get shot. Slim was worried. *What will I do without Ben?* he wondered.

They all remained motionless for several more seconds before Edwin lowered his gun and holstered it. "We'll ride south tomorrow, just like we planned, and that's all there is to it," he declared. "I ain't gonna be caught with stolen gold." With that, he stormed out of the cabin leaving the boys staring at the door. Ben's eyes narrowed as he considered what had just happened, *I'll have to keep a close watch on him.*

Thaddaeus Smith tapped lightly on the door inside the crib with nervous anticipation. The door opened a crack as the girl peered out at her suitor. Suddenly, she threw open the door and exclaimed, "Thaddy!" She happily pulled him inside and leaned down to give him a peck on the cheek. "I was thinking about you all morning, how was church?" she asked with a slight tease.

Hoping she didn't see him blushing in the dimly lit room, he simply replied, "Fine." He sat down on the bed and watched her comb her long, blond hair. "I was hoping that we could take a walk or something."

She turned and slyly asked, "Or something?"

"No, I, um, mean that perhaps supper or something and then a walk."

Pearl giggled at his discomfort before letting him off the hook. "That's sounds nice, let me get my shawl."

The young couple walked slowly along the banks of the Animas River listening to the gurgle of the water as it flowed among the rocks, making its way down the valley. They held hands as they strolled along, quiet, just enjoying each other's company.

Thad was trying to think of something to say to this lovely girl, hoping that she liked him as much as he liked her. The sound of the water made conversation difficult so he led her across a foot bridge and up to the foot of the mountain.

Finding a smooth rock to sit on, they sat down and pulled out some sweet bread that they had brought from the restaurant. Pearl's eyes smiled as she studied the man sitting next to her. She liked what she saw. He was quiet and confident, although shy around girls. He was obviously intelligent and talented and he was always quite the gentleman around her. Pearl hoped that he would think of her as more than just a passing fancy. While most men just came for a quick visit, paying her for her services, Thad seemed interested in her for more than just her body. *I'm falling in love!* she suddenly realized, smiling at the thought.

Thaddaeus munched on some bread while he watched a train pull into the station. From their vantage point overlooking the town, he could see the string of two story buildings along Blair and Greene Streets, single story houses on the west side of town, and all the way up to the smelter. The backdrop of the green, treeless mountain covered in wildflowers with just a hint of snow left on top, made for a picturesque setting. He realized that he was wasting time and turned to the lovely girl sitting next to him.

She was wearing a simple blue dress, modest but still showing off her slim figure. The dress made her pale blue eyes shine and he drank in her beauty as she wiped a crumb from her lips. She had her legs tucked under her, hiding short black boots, boots that made her another inch taller than he, but sitting here on the rock, he could look straight across into her eyes.

Without thinking, he blurted out, "You are beautiful."

Pearl gave a short laugh. She had heard that a hundred times, but she knew he meant it. "Thank you," she answered sweetly as she put a hand on his arm. Moving closer so she could lean against him, she prompted, "Tell me about Chicago."

"That's where I grew up. My father worked for the newspaper and I have two older brothers and a sister. My folks made sure we had a proper education so that we wouldn't have to work on the docks. One brother followed my father in the newspaper business and the other is a lawyer. My sister is married to a doctor and has a baby on the way. As kids, our mother made sure we learned our manners, had us read the Bible each evening, and took us to the park on Sundays."

"What made you become a detective?" she asked.

"I grew up reading about the exploits of the Pinkerton Detectives and I thought it would be fun and adventurous."

"Did your parents approve of you becoming a Pinkerton?" she asked.

"Not really," he replied, "my father wanted me to be a newspaper man as well, but after a while they supported my decision when I showed them some of the cases I had worked on and explained that it takes more intelligence than gunplay to solve a case."

"Is this something that you will continue to do?"

"No," he answered, "I think when I have a family I'll do something different. It can be a dangerous job at times."

"Have you ever killed anyone?"

"Yes, once. There were a couple of men that I shot in the arm or leg to get them to stop, but most of the time, outlaws will give up when you get the drop on them."

"It sounds terribly exciting!" she exclaimed.

"Yes, it can be at times. Sometimes it can be slow when I'm doing paperwork, or just hanging out on a street corner watching a suspect.

"Speaking of watching a suspect, I need to head to town to see what J.T. is doing today. Why don't you come with me?"

"Really?" Pearl asked excitedly.

"Sure, you can help me blend in on Blair Street."

She jumped up, grabbed Thad's hands and pulled him up. "That sounds like fun!" she exclaimed as she threw her arms around him and gave him a big squeeze.

Thad almost lost his mind as he felt her breasts pressed against his chest and inhaled her faint perfume. He started blushing again but quickly grabbed his hat and turned to go to hide his embarrassment. He helped her down from the rock and the two ran down to the foot bridge before making their way across the tracks to find their suspect.

The powder man counted down the seconds, waiting for the blast. All week the drillers had been following a new vein of quartz that branched off from the main lode. Located off the five level shaft, this new vein in the Old Man Mine was large and looked promising from the early samples.

Multiple explosions went off and the powder man tried to count them as best he could. As soon as the dust cleared, several minutes later, muckers moved in to shovel up the rock and load it into the ore cars. Using two man teams, they made short work of the pile of rock and quickly had the ore cars loaded to the top.

A day earlier, the mill had been shut down so the copper screen could be scrapped clean and the stamps serviced. The new ore would be run through without any other product so that an accurate tally could be made of the gold and other metals in the samples. Jackson Ives was hoping for a good return so he could get more money out of the investors and put in a rail line to haul out more ore. The mill just couldn't keep up with the current output of the mine; they had tailing piles growing by the day just outside of the mill. He also needed to improve the tram at the highest levels—the tram towers at the five level were subject to damage from winter snow slides.

With the ore cars full, mules were then used to pull the cars to a vertical shaft where they dumped the ore to a lower level. From there the ore was moved outside to be dumped down a long wooden chute to the tram house. At the tram house, workers shoveled the ore into the tram cars for the long trip down the mountainside where it was dumped directly into the mill.

Gunther Miller oversaw the operation from top to bottom, making sure everything ran smoothly. If there was an accident, work would have to be suspended for an hour or two, which made the owner upset. If the chutes got clogged, a man would have to climb up with a pole and try to pry the rocks free so they could continue on the way, all while trying to keep his arms intact. Whenever a man lost an arm or leg, he usually bled to death before they could get him down to a doctor … causing further delay.

Once a large enough pile had accumulated, Miller gave the order for the mill to start up. The boilers had been stoked and were ready to put on the steam. The large rollers were engaged at the top to start the milling process and then the stamps started pounding the ore into smaller and smaller particles. The thunder from the mill rolled down the valley as the stamps did their job. In a few hours, after the separation process, they would have a sample to rush to the smelter and get the official report of the gold content of the new vein.

J.T. Jones was luxuriating in a hot bath behind the Chinese laundry house. Two girls were scrubbing him clean as he sipped whisky from a small tumbler. "Not too rough on the toes," he chided one girl as she ran a brush along his nails. *This is the life,* he thought as he soaked in the tub. Just a few more train robberies and they could all be off to California to live it up for the rest of their lives. J.T. imagined every day like this—being waited on hand and foot, watching shows, playing poker without caring if he won or lost, and having a whole string of girls for his pleasure. *One for each night of the week,* he thought with a smile.

Thad and Pearl peered through the wood slats of the bathhouse watching the man with the grin. Pearl was trying to stifle a giggle herself as she was amused at their behavior. Thad gave her a warning glare before pulling her back to the street. "We can wait here for him to come out." He looked at his new recruit, "I'm not sure you'd make a good detective," he surmised, "you can't stop giggling!"

Pearl laughed out loud now that they were in the street, "This is fun, sneaking around, spying on folks. But I guess you're right, I can't be quiet."

Over at the station, a whistle blast gave the five minute warning for the afternoon train to Durango. "Let's go look at the train," Thad prompted, "I want to get another look at the mail car."

They quickly ran over to the station and up to the green painted rail car. Thad walked all the way around it, peering underneath and at the ends, trying to figure a way in. Pearl stood at the opened door, watching as someone dropped off a last minute piece of mail. She was looking around the interior as Thad walked up to her side. "What about that?" she asked, pointing to the hatch in the roof.

Thad looked at the hatch skeptically, "It's so small, even a child would be a tight fit."

"What if they use a child?"

Scratching his chin while he thought, Thad tried to size up the hatch before the conductor walked up and slid the door closed. He couldn't imagine using a child but he supposed it was possible. He would have to arrange to have a closer look at the hatch, but not here in Silverton ... he didn't want to alert J.T. or whoever may be watching to the fact that he was investigating.

The locomotive started putting on steam and the couplings clunked as the train started to move. With two long whistle blasts the train pulled away from the station heading down along the river towards Durango.

Thad turned to his new helper and asked her to go back and watch for J.T. "I've got to send a telegram, and then I'll meet up with you." With that he headed into the telegraph office and wrote out a message for Marshal Morton in Durango asking him to measure the hatch on the mail car when it comes through, and then he sent another telegram to the railroad officials in Denver asking them to suspend all shipments of gold for several weeks. It was time to take control of the situation and force the outlaws to show their hand when the time was right - a time that he would pick when everything was in place.

CHAPTER EIGHT

The Old Man Mine was a flurry of new activity. The five level shaft had gone into full production after the favorable assayers reports came back. Two shifts ran day and night; blasting on the night shift and mucking on the day shift. The lesser producing three level had been temporarily shut down so that more men could be put to work on the new strike.

Jackson Ives was meeting with his foreman, discussing several new plans to expand the tram system up to the highest level, and looking at options to increase productivity. Gunther Miller had some reservations about pushing the workers too far. "We've got to give the men a break," Gunther began, "why, just yesterday, Tim Reeves went mad and ran down the four level rock chute. The only thing that stopped him was the pile of rocks at the bottom. He's got two broken legs and the doctor says he may have to amputate. ..."

"I know all that," Ives interrupted, "but we need to keep both shifts running at full strength before winter sets in. Let's get another team of drillers off the four level shaft and see if we can hire some men to start on the new tram towers."

"That'll work as long as I can send two men per shift to go blow off some steam in Silverton during the next few weeks. The last thing we need is for everyone to start going stir-crazy.

Ives looked at his mine foreman for a few seconds and then

conceded. "That's fine; I guess we have to keep the men happy. Give them each a three day pass and have them pull names out of a hat to see who gets to go first. You can also give them their pay, but make sure they know that this'll be it until the end of the year. I need to put everything I have left into the expansion and the investors aren't sending any more cash until they start to see a return on their money."

"What are your plans for the mill?" the foreman asked.

"I'm not sure yet. We don't have any room down in the valley to expand, but I may be able to file a claim on the other side of the creek and build a new mill over there. The other option is to get with Otto Mears and have him run another railroad spur up here so we can start shipping the ore to Durango."

"That would probably be easier," Miller replied.

"Yes, but I'm already over-extended so he may not be willing to do business. Either way, I'll need to get a loan from the bank. I'll let you know by next week and then we'll make plans."

Jackson Ives watched Miller head back to the mine as he contemplated his situation. *If only the investors would send more money*, he thought, *I should never have salted that sample.* He laughed as he thought back. The miner had been killed just the day before when a charge had gone off prematurely. The first thing Miller did before burying the guy was to pull out the gold tooth that the man had been so proud of. It had seemed like fate at the time, but now he wished that he had not tossed it in with the ore sample. The assayers report had shown an uneven balance between the gold and other metals recovered from the ore. Anyone who knew anything about mining could tell that the sample was salted. *Hopefully the investors don't know*, he thought. Ives rubbed his chin as he contemplated all his options. The investors had been shelling out money for over a year now and they wanted to see some profits, or at least a hint of future profits. Ives was sure that the new shaft would pay off soon; he just needed to get some capital to make the needed improvements. *Perhaps the bank will come through*, he hoped. ...

Thaddaeus Ebenezer Smith was reading the newspaper from the day before as he ate his breakfast. Outside, the clouds were gathering as a late summer storm was preparing to drench the region in a few hours. The detective smiled as he read the various stories, still amazed at life here in the "wild west".

The Silverton Standard was now being delivered to his room each day so that he could keep up on the daily activities of the town. After watching some trash being blown down the street, Thad turned back to his reading about two "soiled doves" on Blair Street:

Two unfortunates were reported to have gotten into a scuffle at the Diamond Belle, evening before last, after accusations were made about one girl stealing another's client. The night watchman was called in to separate the two and place them, temporarily, into custody. The two faced Judge Walker and were fined fourteen dollars each plus costs for the incident. Currently, the name of the gentleman is being withheld.

Thad skimmed down the page, reading bits and pieces about activity at the various mines. There were reports of new strikes and others going bust. Amazingly, there were even reports of the exact amounts of gold and silver being produced from not just individual mining companies, but the individual shafts. *At least they aren't reporting when they ship it*, he thought.

Another story about the opium den caught his eye:

A raid last night by the marshal and his watchman at the "dens of the almond-eyed" netted several patrons in various states of stupor, and a Mr. Wong, owner of said establishment, all purported to be now residing in the local jail. The patrons, whose names are being withheld, were released first thing in the morning, while Mr. Wong is being held for trial and is facing considerable fines. A city counselor, name also withheld, stated: "These 'dens of iniquity' need to be shut down permanently and the proprietors should be escorted to the edge of town and asked never to return!" We are reminding our readers that there is still a general boycott of all Chinese establishments in Silverton.

Thad wondered if his suspect was there last night. *I'll have to ask my new sidekick if she saw him this morning,* he thought. He was paying Pearl to act as his eyes and ears when he wasn't around to keep an eye on J.T. So far, she was happy to do the task, and he was happy to have her doing something other than her normal line of work. Thad was starting to have feelings for this girl and he did not want anyone else touching her, and the last thing he wanted to do was to think about such a thing.

After folding up the newspaper and tucking it under his arm, Thad headed for the railroad station to send out a couple of telegrams. One was to the Pinkerton office in Denver and the other was to Marshal Morton in Durango. He was setting the net to capture the outlaws and needed to get some help for the takedown, plus the Marshal in Durango needed to be kept in the loop. It was just a matter of timing to set the trap and to get all the players to follow the plan.

But first things first, he thought. Thad headed over to Blair Street to find Pearl and catch up with her. Plus, he just wanted to see her. He would have a few days before he needed to get down to the serious business of capturing the criminals and he wanted to spend as much time with this girl that he was falling in love with.

A cold wind was sweeping down the street as Thad made his way to the crib and quickly stepped inside. A few spits of rain foretold what was to come in the next hour. He knocked on the door and waited with anticipation.

Pearl cracked open the door and then threw it open when she saw who it was. "My Thaddy!" she exclaimed. "Come in." She pulled him inside and threw her arms around him. Returning her embrace, with just a little less embarrassment than before, Thad greeted her.

"How are you doing this morning? Did you see J.T. last night? Gracious, you look great!" He had just noticed the new dress she was wearing.

"Do you like it?" she asked.

"Absolutely!" he replied as he let his eyes drift along her figure. It was a modest dress that a proper lady would wear, not the attire of a lady of the night. It was light blue with lace around the neck, form fitting around her waist, and then it rippled down and out as it flowed down to her feet. There was also a small bow, tied at the back. He couldn't imagine a more beautiful woman.

"I also got this for you," she said as she pulled out a handkerchief. It was from the same fabric and she folded it expertly and put it in his jacket pocket. "Now we match!" she said with a giggle, and then she leaned forward and gave him a quick peck on the cheek. Pearl stood back and smiled as she gazed at this handsome man, admiring his new look.

Suddenly, without thinking, Thad reached out and pulled her towards him, leaned up slightly and planted a kiss on her soft, subtle lips. He released her just as quickly as they both stood there, somewhat surprised. Thad started to blush as he realized what he had just done, but Pearl just giggled again and gave him a gentle squeeze. "It's about time you did that."

Now suddenly too nervous to try it again, Thad took her by the hand and they sat down on the bed. "Did you see J.T. last night? I read that they raided the opium den."

"No," she replied. "He went out to several of the gambling halls and then was back here around midnight. He does the same thing every night, you know; do you still want me to follow him?"

"No, I have another idea. The next time you run into Jewel, start a conversation with her that you've heard about a large gold shipment going out in a few days."

"What if she asks about where I heard it from?"

"Just tell her one of your clients is the assayer for the Old Man Mine … it's almost the truth!"

They laughed together while they sat there on the bed, holding hands. "What are you going to do next?" Pearl asked.

"I have several stops to make today. I'll be busy for a while so I may not have time to see you today, but I was hoping we could see each other tomorrow?"

"I would like that," she answered softly. "Thad, what's going to happen after you are done here in Silverton?"

He looked into her pale blue eyes, seeing that she was asking a serious question. He started to answer, and then hesitated. It was risking his feelings, to answer her honestly, but he supposed the time was right. "I'll have to leave; head back home to Chicago."

She sat there, looking apprehensively at him, but he held up his hand. "I want you to come with me. …" He said it, and now it was his turn to be worried.

A small tear formed in the corner of her eye as she gave a slight smile. "I would like that," she barely managed to say. But then she threw her arms around him, "Oh Thaddy, you've made me so happy!"

He returned her enthusiastic embrace, thrilled that she wanted the same thing as he. *I'm going to marry the most beautiful woman in the world!*

After mindlessly wandering out into the street, getting drenched by the rain, Pearl ran out the door and threw a slicker around Thad's shoulders and admonished him. "Now keep your mind on the job at hand!"

He knew she was right and he had to make himself concentrate. Wrapping the slicker around his frame, Thad leaned against the driving rain and headed back to the telegraph office.

The late morning train was just pulling out with twenty ore cars headed to the Durango smelters and several empty box cars being returned to Denver. Thad jumped inside the building and shook off the rain. He boldly stepped up to the telegraph operator and showed his Pinkerton badge. "I need to speak with you privately," he declared. The man motioned for him to step around and through the door.

"What can I do for you?" he asked.

"Do you know J.T.? He works at the post office."

"Sure," the man answered, "he comes in every so often."

"Good, now listen. I need you to let me know the next time he sends a telegram. I'm staying at the Grand Hotel, room thirty-one. And don't say anything to anyone about this; it needs to remain confidential."

The telegraph operator assured him that he would comply,

so the detective braved the rain again and headed over to the Greene & Co. Smelter.

George Greene, business owner and co-founder of Silverton, invited the detective to his office to talk privately after Thad had showed the man his badge. The two shook hands as Greene sat behind his desk. "It's good to finally meet the man looking into the gold thefts; we need to get this business taken care of."

"It's nice to meet you as well, Mr. Greene," Thad replied. "I have a fairly good idea of who is behind all this, we just need to catch them in the act in order to prove it … and that's where you come in."

"I'll assist you in any way I can, but I hope it's soon. We've been holding off on shipments like you asked, but our storeroom is getting rich in gold and silver, and we need to get it to Denver. That much bullion sitting in there is making my foreman nervous."

"How much do you think you have right now?" Thad asked.

"Over eighty thousand in gold, thirty in silver." Greene replied. "We'll have twice that amount by the end of the day."

Thad thought for a moment, "That's perfect. I'll need you to send it out for shipment in three days."

"All of it?" Greene asked.

"All of it," Thad answered, "and make sure that J.T. at the post office knows ahead of time that it's coming. Schedule it for the morning train out of Silverton so that it'll be on the evening train by the time it reaches Chama."

George Greene studied this man sitting in front of his desk. "I sure hope you know what you are doing, that is a large amount of money to risk. There is gold in there from four of the area's largest mines, and they are waiting to be paid for it."

"Don't worry about it," Thad assured the man. "Just hire a few more hands to transport it to the train and I'll take care of the rest. Your gold will be safe, and by this time next week, everyone will have been paid."

When Thad stepped outside, the rain was subsiding. There were still dark clouds against the mountains to the east and thunder rippling down through the valley, but the sunlight was shining brightly through from the west. The heat was already causing clouds to form in the valley as the moisture evaporated.

With a skip in his step as he thought about his girl, Thad decided to walk up to the Old Man mine. It was only a few miles, and he was getting used to the altitude. Slinging the slicker across his shoulder, he headed towards Arrastra Gulch, crossing the railroad tracks just after a work train passed, heading south along the Animas to the Silverton Northern rail yard.

Two hours later, after forgetting that it was going to be all uphill, he reached his destination with lungs on fire from the exertion. The mine was a flurry of activity—the tailing pile was growing by the day with the waste from the new shaft, and the mill was thundering as usual with the tons of ore and waste that had been drilled out of the mountain. There were men working all up and down the mountain scurrying all around like so many ants. Thad watched as carpenters started work on the new tram towers which would be perched on the side of the steep cliff, two thousand feet up. Large timbers were cut to size, angled to match the slope, and pre-drilled for the cross-beams to hold it all together. *These men must be half mountain goat*, he thought. He couldn't imagine how they would drag the thousand feet of cable and the eight foot diameter drive wheel up to the top.

After resting for a bit, Thad headed up the stairs to the second floor office of the mine and found Jackson Ives. The man looked five years older than the last time he had seen him. Ives motioned for Thad to follow him to his office. "What can I do for you today?" he asked.

"Do you have any gold to be shipped, or ready to be shipped in the next few days?"

"All I have is sponge waiting for the smelter. Why?" Jackson asked.

"I'm setting a trap for the gold bandits and I wanted to sweeten the pot a bit."

Ives looked beat. "The vein we were following has narrowed and isn't producing. We are going to have to start another shaft or cut deeper into the mountain, hoping that it opens back up."

"Oh," Thad began, "I'm sorry to hear that. You could do me a favor though. ..."

"Whatever I can."

"I need you to let it be known that you are sending a large shipment on the morning train in a few days. It doesn't really matter if it is true or not."

"Who do you want me to tell?"

"Anyone you normally tell, plus just spread it around and let word of mouth do the rest."

Jackson Ives considered that for a moment ... *it'll help if the bank thinks we are doing well, then I'll get the loan I need.* He looked at Thad, "You've got it. I'll start telling folks today and I'll arrange to ship the sponge to Denver."

CHAPTER NINE

Thaddaeus perused the selection of small rings that the proprietor of the general store had laid out. Most were plain bands, either gold or silver, but one ring stood out at the end. "I'd like to see that one," he told the man.

"This is our best ring," the man explained. "One hundred percent Silverton Gold, with a small diamond set at the top and surrounded by two turquoise stones." He leaned closer as if to pass on a secret. "Made by a Ute Indian, but they do excellent work."

Thad glanced at the man, unsure of what that meant, but he decided right away to buy it. The blue turquoise would match her eyes perfectly. *I sure hope she likes it*, he thought.

Returning quickly to the hotel room, Thad put on his best suit, tied a perfect knot on his tie, and made sure the blue handkerchief was in his jacket pocket. He put on his derby hat and headed out to find his girl.

The sun was shining brightly on this late summer morning as Thad walked down Blair Street. He had a skip in his step as he approached the crib where Pearl worked. They had planned an outing up to the town of Eureka so they could enjoy the day together.

Once again, Thad had a moment of nervousness as he tapped on her door. It faded quickly as the door opened and there she was, dressed in her new blue dress, smiling at him, beautiful as ever. Thad smiled back, "Are you ready?" he asked as he held out his arm.

"Yes," she replied excitedly. Pearl had not been away from town since she had arrived in Silverton. She leaned down to give him a peck on the cheek and took his arm as they made their way to the train station. "You look very nice today," she said as she pretended to adjust his new handkerchief.

Beaming proudly, walking arm in arm, the couple headed toward the train station. The Silverton Northern was still under construction, but they were going to ride as far as possible, and then take a wagon up to the small mining town of Eureka.

The old Baldwin 4-4-0 locomotive sat waiting at the siding with a full head of steam, creaking and hissing, ready to make the short trip north. The train had just one passenger car and several flat cars loaded with construction equipment and supplies. Most of the passengers were Italian workers heading up to the end of the line, preparing to lay the next bit of track to make it to Eureka and beyond.

The couple sat in the back, away from the staring eyes of the workers. Thad wondered briefly if any of these men had been one of her customers, but he quickly expelled the thought from his mind. That was her previous life and it didn't matter anymore.

Pearl took the window seat, eagerly awaiting the trip. Silverton had been like a prison after her husband had died, holding her in town because of her profession. But all that was about to change—this man sitting beside her was going to take her away from all her troubles.

After two long blasts from the whistle, the engineer released the brakes and applied the throttle as the train pulled away from the station. Slowly gaining speed, the locomotive worked its way along the Animas River. They made several stops along the way, picking up and dropping off workers for the mines and railroad. Thad and Pearl ignored them all, engrossed in each other's company and enjoying the ride. The mountains loomed large on either side of the river valley, towering thousands of feet on either side. Every so often, you could see a small stream cascading down the mountainside and into the Animas. There were small mineshafts everywhere they looked, easy to pick out with the tailing pile in front of the hole. As they passed, marmots scurried down the rocks to a safe burrow after giving a chirp of warning to fellow animals. Pearl giggled as she pointed them out to Thad, laughing at their fat little bodies as they ran.

All too soon, they reached the end of the line. Thad jumped down off the step and turned around to help Pearl step down. They walked up past the locomotive as it hissed away excess steam and looked for a wagon to hire. "It's only half a mile to Eureka," one of the workers told them, so they decided to walk the rest of the way.

Taking her hand, Thad led her up the path as they made their way towards town. Soon it was quiet and they were all alone. A hummingbird zoomed past as they walked beside a field of wildflowers up along the hillside. "It's so beautiful," Pearl exclaimed.

Thad was having a difficult time seeing the beauty beyond his love. His hands were sweating and he was getting nervous. It was now or never. Thad stopped walking, spun around in front of her and dropped to one knee. "Pearl, will you marry me?"

She opened her mouth in surprise and happy shock and was about to answer when he interrupted her. "Oh wait, I forgot something." He stood back up and fished around in his pocket before finding the ring. "Here," he said, holding it out to her.

Her eyes went wide as she saw the ring with the diamond sparkling in the sunlight. "Oh, Thaddy, it's wonderful!" Pearl held out her hand so he could slip it on her finger. He grinned with delight as he saw his ring on her hand.

"Is that a yes, then?"

"Oh, yes! Absolutely!" Pearl threw her arms around her man and kissed him and then kissed him again. This was the most wonderful day of her life!

Slim ran full force through the door of the little cabin, waving a piece of paper. "It's a telegram from J.T." Ben snatched it away from him and quickly scanned through it. They used code words whenever sending a telegram since it could be read by others, but the message was clear.

"The largest shipment of the season is going out in two days. J.T. says it'll most likely be worth over one hundred thousand dollars!"

"Will it be the right train?" Edwin asked.

"Yeah," Ben replied, "the night train—perfect!"

Edwin scratched his chin while he thought. "This will be the big one, our last job. We'll take every ounce of gold off that train and then head for California. Ben, you make sure to get some more mules so we can haul the extra weight. Slim, you start packin', and make sure we have enough food for a week. I'll head to town and send a note to J.T. to make sure he is on that train and ready to run."

The noon train had just arrived in Durango, pulling three passenger coaches and several freight cars. Two tough looking men stepped down, each carrying a Winchester rifle and a Colt strapped to their side. They disappeared through the crowd gathered at the station and walked briskly towards the end of town, turning only when they reached the jailhouse.

Town Marshal Morton sat at his desk, feet propped up, appearing to be asleep. He could tell immediately who these men were just from the way they handled themselves. Moreover, he knew that they were coming. Morton pushed his Stetson back on his head and greeted the newcomers. "Detective Thaddaeus whatever-his-name-is told me to expect you, gentlemen. Anything you need, just let me know."

"We just need a place to sleep and someone to get us on that evening train, when the time comes."

"Consider it done," Morton said. With that he led the two Pinkerton Detectives back to the jail and offered them a couple of bunks to sleep on. "I'll have dinner brought in for you, if you like, and I'll make sure you're on that train day after next."

The newly engaged couple almost ran into Eureka, giddy with excitement. Pearl kept looking at her new ring and then at her fiancé, equally happy with both. She smiled at each as they walked to the collection of buildings. The small town of Eureka was still like a frontier town with log cabins and hastily built frame buildings scattered haphazardly around. The two planned to get a meal and then just wander around until it was time to return on the late train.

They found a boarding house, a cabin with a tent roof, which was serving lunch. The only item on the menu was steak with beans so that was what they ate, washing it down with some strong, bad coffee.

Ignoring their surroundings, the two ate in silence, gazing into each other's eyes. As soon as they were finished, Thad led her outside and they strolled around the buildings and then up a side canyon called Eureka Gulch. At the top of the gulch lay another huge mine called the Sunnyside, but they knew it would take too long to hike that far, so they were content to sit by the small creek cascading down the canyon.

"When do you want to get married?" she asked.

Although tempted to say "Right now!" Thad suggested they should get married as soon as they got back to Chicago. "I want to be able to have my parents in attendance."

"I can't wait to meet them, and your siblings too. Oh, Thaddy, I'm so happy!" She leaned forward and waited for him to kiss her again, which he gladly did. Her lips were soft and lush and he suddenly wished that he could do more. Thad pulled her close and felt her body against his, warm and soft, but he was going to respect this girl and do the right thing until they were properly married, so he reluctantly pushed her away.

They sat down next to the creek and kissed some more and talked about everything under the sun … well, mostly she talked while he listened. She told him about her past and how she had ended up in Silverton, then she told him about her sad life on Blair Street doing what she had to do to survive. Next, she shared about her dreams of being married again and having a family someday. When she was through, they just sat there, suddenly quiet, simply enjoying each other's presence for a while.

The wagon, heavy with guards and gold, slowly traveled down Greene Street. Tiny, with shotgun in hand, led the way as the procession purposely passed the bank before turning back and heading over towards the train station. Jackson Ives had hired extra men just for this little show he was putting on. Four men, armed to the teeth, followed the wagon. Both Ives and his foreman rode alongside just to make sure that everyone in town saw him and knew the wagon was from the Old Man Mine.

The freight wagon was loaded with bags of unrefined gold sponge being sent all the way to Denver for processing. Ives was hoping that the results from the assayers report on this new batch would prove to be valuable. If everything worked out, he could pay back his loan, pay off the investors, and make the payroll for the workers. After that, with new investments, he could continue with improvements and expansion of the mine. Jackson Ives felt that with one big, last push up through the vein, he could make millions over the next ten years. *After that, I'll sell out and retire*, he thought, *and maybe even sooner.*

The men pulled up alongside a specially prepared baggage and mail car sitting on a siding next to the station. The heavy bags were offloaded from the wagon and transferred to the mail car. The armed guards then took up station along the tracks and would stay until the rail car was on its way. Shipping this way was unprecedented—usually, packages of small ingots were shipped discreetly, one or two at a time, in the mail. Sending a large shipment all at once with all this fanfare was generating a lot of excitement and attention.

As Ives rode back towards his mine, he was both worried and confident that his plan would work. *After all, the vein had been producing for years, why would it give out now? I'll head to the Silverton bank tomorrow and secure a new loan.* Satisfied that all was in order, Jackson nudged his horse into a canter and headed toward home.

In the telegraph office, the operator wrote down a series of letters as they ticked off on the keypad. Normally, he didn't pay any attention to the words, but this time he took special note. It was addressed to J.T. and the message didn't make much sense. With hurried importance, the operator made a second copy and ran out to deliver the messages. Conveniently, both went to the same building. He passed the first copy to J.T. as he sat behind his desk in the lobby of the Grand Hotel, then he ran up the stairs and slipped the second copy under the door of number thirty-one. *I sure hope that detective knows what it means*, he thought.

When Thad and Pearl returned to the crib after their excursion, Jewel met them at the door. "Where have you been?" she exploded, "There have been clients asking for you all week!"

Pearl ignored her anger and held out her hand for inspection. "Look, I'm getting married!" She then introduced her fiancé, "This is Thaddaeus Ebenezer Smith, from Chicago."

"Pleased to meet you," Thad said, tipping his hat.

Jewel looked him up and down and immediately dismissed him. She turned back to Pearl and demanded her payment for the week.

"I'll be leaving in a few days," Pearl said. "I'll pay you before I leave." With that, the two went inside to say goodnight, leaving a fuming Jewel glaring at the closed door.

It was well after midnight as Thaddaeus finally put down his notes. Reading in bed, he poured over the telegram from Chama as well as one that J.T. had sent earlier. The code words used in the messages were similar and obviously were discussing the same subject matter.

Inserting his own words "gold" and "train" in various places, as well as some other words, he was, after several hours, able to decipher the entire message. The outlaws were definitely planning to hit the eastbound train on Friday. If all went according to plan, he, and his help, could take down the entire gang when they struck.

Leaning back on his pillow, Thad reviewed the plan in his mind. Had he allowed for every eventuality? The plan was simple, really. Simple meant that there was less that could go wrong. He reached over and turned down the lamp, confident that everything was in order. Tomorrow, he would check his supplies, review the plan once more and then spend some more time with Pearl. He would then get plenty of sleep in preparation for the big day.

CHAPTER TEN

Friday morning found Thad up and packing his gear before sunrise. His carpetbag was lighter than when he had arrived as his .45 Colt was tucked behind his back, and the derringer was hiding, out of sight, in his boot. One of his knives was held in a small scabbard on his belt, and the trusty Hopkins Allen revolver was in its usual place, in the shoulder holster, under his arm. Using his brain had gotten him this far, but now, he needed to be ready for anything, including gunplay. Thad was up to the task; his role as a Pinkerton required him to be able to use a gun and use it well, and never to back down from a fight. This was serious work and he was going to see it completed.

Heading downstairs, the Detective handed in his room key and went out into the street to find some breakfast. Dim light silhouetted the mountain peaks to the east while the cold night air suggested that winter was not too far off. Thad pulled his jacket tighter and found a small kitchen that was just getting started. He ordered steak and eggs and slowly ate while gazing out of the window at the deserted street. Off in the distance, a rooster crowed, anticipating the rising sun, while a mangy dog slinked past, down the alley, drawn by the smell of bacon frying in the kitchen.

Thad contemplated his time here in this high mountain town. He was constantly amazed at life here in Silverton and thought to himself that it might make a good place to live ... someday. *Although, the winters can be harsh*, he reminded himself. There were some years that the snowfall was so deep that the trains couldn't get up here from Durango and the town was cut off for months. But he was used to harsh winters in Chicago ... surely he could handle it.

A train whistle interrupted his thoughts. He checked his pocket watch and downed the last of his coffee. After leaving a few coins on the table, he hurried over to the train station. Gazing at the sky as he walked, Thad noticed clouds already gathering over the western peaks. *Another storm is coming*, he thought, *this could be a problem*. He shrugged it off knowing that there was nothing anyone could do about the weather. He felt for the reassuring bulk of the gun under his arm and then reached into his pocket for his ticket, having purchased it the day before to make sure he had a seat on the train.

There was a flurry of activity at the train station and around the siding next to the main track. A yard engine was moving the mail car into position on the main line, positioning it in front of another baggage car and three passenger coaches. A 2-6-0 Mogul locomotive had just taken on a full load of coal and water and moved into position. The fireman was shoveling coal into the firebox as the locomotive built up a full head of steam, preparing for the long trip to Durango, Chama, and then Antonito.

Passengers were saying farewell to friends and family, porters were overseeing the loading of luggage and large travel trunks, and the brakeman was making his final inspections before the scheduled departure.

Pearl was standing in front of Thad with a worried look on her face as he tried to reassure her. "We've got the element of surprise, nothing will go wrong. I know what I'm doing."

"I know," she replied, still not totally convinced. She wiped a small tear away and gave her man a quick hug and a peck on the cheek. After straightening his tie again, they said goodbye. She waved as he turned around to look at her again and then he disappeared inside.

At the other end of the platform, Jewel turned back to J.T. with a questioning look. "I thought those two were getting married. Why do you suppose she isn't going with him?"

J.T. shrugged his shoulders as he picked up his bag. "Don't worry about them, worry about us. I'll send for you when I get settled." With that he jumped up onto the step and went inside, leaving Jewel staring after him. He had no intention of sending for her, he was going to find a new girlfriend, or two, after they got to California. *That girl is too old and bitter*, he decided.

J.T. took his seat and caught a glimpse of Pearl's fiancé. Thad had waited for J.T. to take his seat before settling down a few rows back and on the other side. With a sudden nagging thought, J.T. wondered who this man was. It did seem strange that he was leaving alone, and on the same train. But it was going to be a long trip back to Chama so he ignored the thought and leaned his head against the window frame as he tried to get some more sleep. *Besides, no one knows who I am*, he reassured himself.

As the engineer applied pressure to the throttle, the train slowly rolled forward with little effort as the entire trip was downhill. Thad waved out of the window at the most beautiful girl in the world as she smiled and waved back. Pearl ran down the length of the platform waving until she reached the edge and had to stop. As she stopped to catch her breath, she saw Thad lean out of the window, tip his hat to her, and threw her a kiss. Her heart stopped for a moment as she fell in love with him all over again. *I can't wait for him to get back!* she thought.

Just then, as she turned to go, Jewel stood in front of her, blocking her path. "Why aren't you goin' with him?" she demanded. "Did he leave you? I told you it wouldn't last."

Pearl had suddenly had enough of this woman who had run her life for the past year. "He's going to go arrest the men who have been stealing gold off this train, including your boyfriend!"

"You whoring hussy!" Jewel screamed as she lunged out at Pearl.

The two girls started screaming and fighting right there on the train platform as onlookers watched in amazement and amusement. Jewel scratched at Pearl's eyes while she pulled her hair. The two fell to the ground, wrestling while everyone watched the fight.

Suddenly, the town marshal ran up and pulled the two girls apart. Both had ripped dresses and dirt that covered them from head to toe. Pearl had a nasty looking scratch down one side of her face while Jewel was missing an entire patch of hair.

The marshal was hauling both girls over to the jail while the crowd laughed and pointed, re-telling the story for those who had missed it. "Just the reason those soiled doves need to stay on Blair Street," one man told another.

As the crowd dispersed, Mr. Hung, owner of the Chinese laundry and other establishments, walked out from behind a shipping crate where he had overheard the conversation between the girls. He padded quietly inside and requested to send a telegram to Chama. J.T. was one of his best clients and he wanted to continue to take his money, as it seemed there was an endless supply of it. He just hoped it wasn't too late.

Then, two minutes later, after Mr. Hung had left, the telegraph operator sent a second telegram to the Chama office.

Thaddaeus Smith spent the trip to Durango switching

between reading the newspaper, watching his suspect, and gazing at the remarkable scenery. As the train followed the Animas River south, the air grew warmer and the mountains grew lower as they approached their destination. A brief rain shower drenched the train just before they made a quick stop in Hermosa, promising more to come later in the day. Thad didn't expect any action before they reached Chama, but he was alert and ready for anything, should the need arise. J.T., however, spent most of the trip trying to get some sleep and only once glanced back around at the small man sitting a few rows behind.

Three hours after they left, the train rolled into Durango. The streets were hot and dusty, a drastic change to the cool mountain air of Silverton. Most of the passengers disembarked as there would be a thirty minute delay before the train continued on its way.

Thad watched J.T. for a few minutes, just long enough to see that he was only hanging out at the station for the break. He used his diminutive size to his advantage and disappeared into the crowd. Walking down a back alley, he headed over to the jail and slipped inside. Marshal Morton and the two Pinkerton men were busy checking their guns for the upcoming action.

Out of the corner of his eye, Morton saw Thad enter. He immediately recognized the short detective. "Are we still set to go with this plan of yours, Mr. Smith?" he asked.

Thad smiled at the man's craftiness, "Hello Marshal. Yes, everything is in place, and I've confirmed that they will go for the gold this evening. Are you gentlemen ready to go?"

"Yep. Just tell us what you want to do."

"All right, the mail car is open for business as usual. Just get in line and wait for my signal. When I raise my hat, you two jump on board. After that, you know what to do."

The two simply nodded and then they all gathered their gear

and headed for the station. The four men took different directions down the street to avoid drawing attention to themselves and then they mixed in with the crowd gathered around the eastbound train.

Thad waited until the marshal took up position next to the open door on the mail car and watched as the two Pinkerton Detectives inched forward in line. Then, as they were in place, Thad walked up to J.T., who was still lounging in the same spot, and distracted him. "Sure is hot here in Durango," he began as he lifted his hat, "I miss the cool air of the mountains."

J.T. looked down at the little man and was about to say something when the train whistle blew. Thad replaced his derby and turned back towards the train. "Time to board," he yelled over his shoulder as he walked away. He glanced over towards the mail car and all three lawmen were out of sight. Thad boarded the coach satisfied that all was going according to plan.

The ride to Chama was uneventful, just like the trip down from Silverton; however, Thad was alert as they drew closer to the small town. At this point, he was unsure whether the bandits would hit right before or just after the train was in Chama.

By the time they reached Chama, Thad was getting tired. The trip had taken all afternoon as the train had stopped at several small towns along the way, picking up passengers and delivering mail that had been sorted along the way inside of the mail car. It would be good to get out and walk around a bit before the next part of the journey.

As the train pulled in from the south side of town, Thad knew that the robbery would occur on the uphill part of the trip. *Makes sense*, he thought, *the train travels slower going up the mountain.*

After disembarking, Thad walked around the station and watched as the workers added a Pullman sleeper car to the train. Those with the money could pay extra to sleep for the overnight run all the way up to Alamosa. From there, the tracks were standard gauge and all the passengers had to switch to another train for the remainder of the trip up to Denver.

The rail yard was a buzz of activity. A 2-8-0 Baldwin helper locomotive was brought into place in front of the Mogul for the long uphill climb, and the mail car was closed and locked after all the mail had been loaded. A long blast of the whistle followed by a short one signaled the train was ready to pull out.

Thad joined his fellow travelers and boarded the train. He took the same spot just a few seats behind his suspect and prepared for the job at hand. The train jolted as the men tested the brakes just before heading out. Just then, a man jumped into the passenger car and started reading out several names. J.T. raised his hand as the telegraph operator handed him a message. When his own name was read out, Thaddaeus did the same. He watched J.T. as he read his telegram and saw the man stiffen. He looked down at his own telegram and quickly read it: *J.T. has been warned about you,* was all it said, but it was enough. He looked up to see the bandit staring back at him through narrowed eyes. *He knows, but he doesn't know that I know,* he thought.

J.T. stood up suddenly but the train started to move, throwing him back down in his seat. It was too late, there was no way to warn his brothers. As he sat there, feeling the train move faster towards the mountains, he started to plan what he would have to do. The only way he could help his family now would be to take care of this lawman before they jumped on the train. He felt for the revolver in his jacket pocket and waited for the right moment.

Thad stared at the message in his hand for several moments. What would this mean? What would J.T. do now? He still had the advantage sitting behind the outlaw, and J.T. didn't have the opportunity to warn the other members of his gang, so nothing had changed, he hoped. It was going to be a long trip up the mountain.

CHAPTER ELEVEN

The two locomotives chugged up the steep grade as the firemen threw in shovelful after shovelful of coal. The fire was roaring, keeping the boiler at full steam, allowing the engineer to keep the train at full power. Thick, black smoke poured out of the stack as the train pounded up the mountain towards Cumbres Pass.

Thad sat on the edge of his seat, watching his quarry. He ignored the sudden late afternoon rain shower that was pelting the side of the train, instead, he sat alert, ready for action. J.T. had been getting more and more restless, twitching in his seat, indicating that he was getting ready to make his move. *We must be getting close to the spot,* Thad reasoned. He reached up to feel his jacket for the hundredth time just to make sure it was open and ready for quick access to the gun.

The train had just entered "The Narrows" when Thad saw J.T. check his watch. The Pinkerton Detective licked his lips and waited, knowing that it was going to happen anytime now. Just then, J.T. turned his head slightly and Thad knew it was coming. Jumping up out of his seat, J.T. reached into his jacket pocket for his Colt. One second ahead of him, Thad reached under his arm and drew the Hopkins. He was already pointing it at J.T. when the outlaw turned around. Stunned, J.T. couldn't believe it when he saw a gun aimed in his direction by that little man. Thad yelled for him to drop the gun, but just then the man sitting in front of Thad stood up. "What's going on here?" he demanded.

With the detective suddenly blocked from view, J.T. fired, hitting the man who had interrupted, grazing him in the head. Several folks screamed and most dove for the floor. Thad swore under his breath and pushed the wounded man down on his seat. He raised the gun and fired, but J.T. was already making for the door. The bullet missed and plowed into the wood paneling of the coach, but Thad was already firing again at the fleeing man. J.T. felt the second bullet buzz next to his ear as he was trying to open the door. He turned to fire but couldn't see his target. Having taken cover behind the bench seat, Thad fired his third shot carefully, hitting the outlaw in the arm that was holding the Colt. If J.T. had simply run out of the door, he may have gotten away, but instead he had turned to try and return fire, sealing his fate. As soon as the bullet hit his arm, he dropped the gun as the pain shot down to his fingers.

"Give it up!" Thad yelled at the bandit as he walked forward. He eased back the hammer on the Hopkins putting visual force behind his words.

J.T. looked down at the Colt for a second, trying to decide if he could go for it with his other hand, but he knew he had been beat. Despite the pain in his arm, he raised his hands in surrender and turned around when Thad motioned. The detective pulled out a set of handcuffs and locked them securely on the outlaw. "See to the wounded," he shouted to the other passengers as he went for the door. There was still a gold heist to stop.

Ben and Slim were sitting on the rock, just like before, except this time they were getting drenched. The downpour had lasted for twenty minutes, soaking them clean through. Edwin watched from a distance laughing. He was dressed in a slicker which kept off the rain, but the boys had to be ready to jump and couldn't wear the long coats. As usual, Edwin held the extra horses and would meet up with the boys up at the pass. Earlier, they had left the mules tied up near the lake so they could be used to haul the loot as well as a week's worth of supplies as they went on the run.

Ben nudged Slim as he heard the train approach. Amazingly, Slim had been asleep, unconcerned as usual, and seemingly unaffected by the rain. "Get ready!" he hissed at his brother.

Slim grabbed his gear and crouched down next to the rock, ready to jump. The two locomotives came into view as they rounded the corner pulling the two baggage cars, several passenger coaches, and two sleeper cars. The train was moving slow and Ben knew that even with the rain, the jump would be easy. *Too bad this'll be the last time*, he thought, *we're really getting the hang of this.*

The two boys were engulfed in smoke as the locomotives passed and then it was time. Ben slapped Slim on the back and the two made the jump. They quickly crawled forward and found the hatch. Using the pry bar, they forced open the hatch and threw the latch. It was dark inside just like it should be so Slim threw in his bag and then squeezed down inside, scraping his narrow shoulders on the way.

Pulling out a match, Slim found the lantern and lit it. As he hung it back on the wall, he looked around the now familiar layout. The safe was sitting in the middle with the mail sorting desk at one end. The other end of the car was piled high with bags of mail and ore sacks. As his eyes adjusted to the light, he could see something else behind the sacks. Slim's mouth dropped open as he heard the unmistakable sound of a

Winchester being cocked. "Reach for the sky, boy, you're under arrest!"

Slim threw his long arms up to the roof and looked up at the hatch to try and warn Ben but his mouth wouldn't work. But it didn't matter. Ben had heard the command and threw closed the hatch as he turned to run.

Inside, the second Pinkerton listened to the sound of footsteps across the roof and started firing. Several rounds followed Ben as he raced down to the end of the car as the lawman levered in one round after another, the concussion and gun smoke filling the enclosed rail car. One bullet managed to clip Ben's boot but it was too late. He jumped to the second baggage car and kept running.

From the platform of the passenger coach, Thad had found the ladder leading to the roof and had climbed most of the way up. From this vantage point he had seen the outlaws jump onto the train. *So they did use the hatch!* he thought. *Pearl was right.* He smiled at the thought of her before shaking his head clear. One of the bandits was running down the length of the train right for him.

Grabbing the top rung of the ladder, Thad pulled himself up and jumped up to the top of the car. Ben spotted him immediately and skidded to a halt, bracing himself against the rocking motion of the train. He reached for the revolver in his holster, but it was still tied down. As he fumbled to release the gun, Thad pulled his Hopkins Allen and pulled the trigger. The gun bucked in his hand but the shot missed! The motion of the train had thrown off his aim. Just then, Ben pulled his Colt but he also fired too quickly, the bullet just missing his target. Frightened into action, Thad fired again. This time he was closer, but he still missed, and there was another problem—he was out of bullets. Thad thought he was done for unless he could pull the .45 from his waistband.

Twenty feet away, the bandit had a slight grin on his face. He could tell that the man standing on the other car was out of shots. Taking careful aim, Ben pulled back the hammer and squeezed the trigger. But just as he fired, a bolt of lightning struck, so close that the thunder clap was only a split second behind, causing him to jump, and threw off his aim. The shot missed! The air was full of electricity as Thad dove for the roof of the car and pulled his backup. The big gun bucked in his hand twice as he shot the stunned outlaw square in the chest. Ben slumped to his knees and slowly buckled to the roof, his life draining away as he took his final breath. Thad breathed a sigh of relief as he rolled over onto his back. Another close lightning strike spurred him back into action and he ran forward to make sure that all was well inside the mail car.

As the train pulled in to Lobato station, curious passengers, ignoring the persistent drizzle, stuck their heads out of the windows to try and see what had happened. The porter opened the mail car as the two Pinkertons escorted Slim out into the open, prodding him along with the business end of their Winchesters. Thad found himself looking at the skinniest man he had ever seen. It was now easier to see how they had been able to use the hatch. Slim was crying and unsure of what to do. When they lowered Ben's body off of the roof, Slim collapsed to the ground, sobbing. "What am I going to do?" he wailed. Thad had gone inside and collected J.T. and paraded him down at gunpoint to join the others. It had been decided to send the gang to Denver to face federal charges and the two Pinkerton agents would escort them there. Thad would remain here to clean up any loose ends. Slim continued to weep as one of the bystanders suggested to him that he would be spending the next twenty years in prison.

Up on the hill, just above the Lobato siding, Edwin slammed shut his looking glass and jammed it into his saddlebag. "Damn fool boys, gettin' caught like that!" He cursed under his breath for a while before gathering the horses. *Guess I'll have to spend all that money by myself*, he thought as he rode up to the lake to collect the supplies. "I ain't goin' back to jail," he told the horse as he rode away.

The following day, after borrowing a horse in Chama, and finding an Indian tracker, Thad rode up along the railroad tracks to look for clues. He had a nagging thought that there had to be another member of the gang. The folks in Chama thought that they had seen Slim with two other men but no one was exactly sure. *It makes sense though*, he thought as they rode along the tracks. Someone had to meet them before and after the robberies had taken place.

The Ute who was helping track silently pointed to a faint trail leading up along the rocks above the tracks. It was in the right place where Thad had seen the men jump, at least as best as he could remember in the heat of the action. There were scuff marks on the rocks indicating that someone had spent some time there, but there was no other sign. The rain had washed away any tracks for them to follow. The two rode up as far as Cumbres Pass and scouted around. After several hours and no luck, they came across several mules tied up to a tree. Thad got down off his horse and examined the animals. Each had a pair of large saddlebags which were empty. "Left them here since he didn't need them after his boys were caught," he told the Indian.

There were more signs indicating that there had been

additional mules here, but with the washed out mud, it was impossible to determine which direction they had gone. With little else to do, the two rode back to Chama so Thad could send a report. With most of the previous thefts of gold still missing, folks were not going to be happy. J.T. and Slim weren't talking and their brother was dead. At this point, the only money accounted for was the hundreds of dollars J.T. spent at the gambling halls in Silverton. The only consolation was the fact that the bandits had been caught and he had finished his job. It was time to head back to Silverton and collect his girl.

CHAPTER TWELVE

The steps of the courthouse were full of people. The San Juan County Sheriff was conducting an auction as directed by the court. Several items of value were being sold to raise funds for delinquent loans and failed businesses. Most were smaller items such as a boiler, a three stamp mill, and a couple of buildings in town. However, most folks had shown up to see how much the Old Man Mine would bring. One of the largest and most successful mines in the area, the Old Man had been producing for years and most thought it would never play out, but with payroll due and Jackson Ives overextended and nowhere to find new funds, the mine had declared bankruptcy and had to be sold.

The defeated Ives stood at the back of the crowd, sadly staring at the ground. No one locally, especially the local bank, had been fooled by the falsified assayers report, and it certainly didn't help that the Silverton Standard wrote a scathing editorial about the possibility of a salted ore sample, and the three hundred thousand needed to expand the mine just wasn't there. Ives simply hoped that someone would step forward with enough to bail him out. He had posted notices in newspapers all over the country advertising the sale. If there was someone foolish enough, *or ignorant enough*, he thought, then his troubles would be over.

The bidding had started and as expected the number started out low. Twenty, then thirty thousand was called out. Jackson looked around at the bidders. Most were from out of town, here just for the auction, or agents for out-of-town bidders. Suddenly, someone bumped the bid up to fifty thousand, garnering some applause. Looking over to his left, Ives spotted a man, dressed in a tweed suit, smiling from ear to ear. In his hand he held a newspaper showing the ad that Jackson had placed and his other hand was still in the air, certain that his bid would win. The man had stars in his eyes as he imagined owning a gold mine. The ore sample had been authenticated ... after all, the report had been done by the best firm in Denver, and several of his friends in New York were willing to risk all to own it with him. He would simply hire the current owner to run it for him and they could all sit back and enjoy the profits!

Another bid was placed causing the man to scowl. He quickly bid seventy and then had to go up another twenty thousand. He started to worry; this was getting close to their limit. This was his last chance. "One hundred thousand!" he declared. There was a buzz of excitement going through the crowd. Jackson Ives held his breath as he waited for another bid.

"Sold!" the sheriff shouted as the crowd clapped and congratulated the new owner. Ives smiled as he walked away. There was enough money to pay his debt to the bank and for him to retire somewhere where no one could find him. The investors were simply out of luck, and the new owner would have to deal with the workers.

The Cow Boy Band, just in from Dodge City, started playing *Color Guard March* as the auction finished and folks started to disperse. There was going to be fun and entertainment all day due to the fact that the electric lights were going to be turned on for the first time this evening.

Thad took Pearl by the arm and led her away from the courthouse where they had been watching the auction. "What would you like to do now?" he asked as they headed down Greene Street.

Pearl was so giddy, she could barely contain herself. It was like a holiday in Silverton today with all the festivities planned. "Let's get something to eat and then we can watch the parade!"

Smiling at her enthusiasm, Thad wanted to tell her how excited he was that she was going to be his wife, but he was still bashful talking to her. It was easier to enjoy the sites and activities than to talk—he simply reveled being in her presence. They still received some disapproving scowls from folks, especially the "proper" women of the town, but most tolerated the relationship. It did help that most of the townsfolk knew that he was responsible for the takedown of the gold thieves, but it was still known that he was going to marry a former prostitute. If it hadn't been for that fact, Thad would have considered staying there in that high mountain town. The more time he spent there, the more he liked it. The people, the industrious spirit, and the scenery made for an idyllic setting. Of course, he still had to remind himself that life there during winter was harsh. But then he started to think about someone who could keep him warm in winter and he started to blush.

"Thaddy!" she interrupted his thoughts, "what do you want to eat?"

He looked over the choices from the street vendor and picked "Venison-on-a-Stick", following her lead. They took a seat in front of the Metropolitan Saloon and watched as the band marched down the street. The band members led the parade with their banner and a pair of longhorn cattle horns, and they were almost drowned out by the cheering of the crowd as they passed. The band was followed by the workers on the electric light project and the owners of the generating station, then the town council and the town marshal marched by. Several children ran past, following the parade, pretending they were part of the event. Pearl giggled as she watched them and Thad watched her as he munched on his lunch.

She turned to him suddenly. "Let's go watch the fight next!"

Thad laughed and agreed ... never to be surprised by this Silverton girl and her amazing spirit. He thought about the comment the storekeeper made and changed it slightly for his own thoughts. *She is my Silverton Gold!*

He grabbed her hand and they made their way over to Blair Street to watch the fight. It was a professional bout, brought in just for this occasion. Two undefeated heavyweights were set to spar for this prizefight. It started slowly, after the bell rang, the two bare-knuckle fighters circling, throwing a short jab or two, trying to feel each other out. Two, and then three rounds went on like this before the crowd started to boo and hiss in complaint. Then, in the next round, one of the fighters threw a huge punch to his opponents face, knocking out a tooth and spraying blood across the rink. The crowd cheered as the fight was on. Angered, the other fighter stepped in and started pounding his adversary's body with hit after hit. The two went on for several more rounds before one of them hit the ground, unconscious after a sharp jab to his jaw. The referee made the count and declared the winner.

There were several more contests planned, all of which Pearl wanted to watch. First, there was a horse race which was followed by a foot race, then, much to the amusement of all, an ore cart race. The final contest, which Thad found the most interesting, was a drilling race. Six teams had been selected and six boulders had been brought in for the contest. Each team had two men swinging sledgehammers and one man to handle the drill. When the pistol was fired, the teams started swinging, trying to get the drill into the rock as far as possible. The crowd was shouting encouragement and rooting for whichever team they had placed a bet on. Thad watched in amazement as the drill dug further and further into the rock. He could see now how some of the tunnels in the Old Man Mine went back for thousands of feet. Another pistol shot rang out and the men stopped swinging, exhausted by the event. The man holding the drill was covered in dust and Thad wondered how he still had all his fingers. Next, each hole was measured and the winners announced, each man receiving a bar of pure silver from a nearby mine. The crowd applauded the efforts of all and then grudgingly exchanged money from losers to winners.

Finally worn out from the activities of the day, the couple retired to a restaurant for dinner. They would have an early meal before boarding the evening train to Durango. After a week of wrapping up loose ends, and paying a fine to get his girl out of jail, Thad was ready to take his fiancée home.

As they sat quietly after the meal, Pearl gazed at her ring then looked at Thad. "I have something I need to tell you."

He looked into her eyes, suddenly worried. "What is it?"

"My name isn't Pearl. That's just the name I used while working on the line."

Thad let out a breath of air, relieved. "That's all right," he said. "What is your name?"

She took a breath of her own, hoping that he liked it. "Kimberly Elizabeth Muller."

Thad almost shouted for joy, "Why, that's a wonderful name! It's full and long and something to be proud of!"

Kimberly reached for his hands and held them tight. The two laughed together. "Well, Thaddaeus Ebenezer Smith, I think we should be getting to our train."

Far to the west, in San Francisco, a scruffy old man wearing a brand new suit and the finest boots money could buy, sat in the parlor of the fanciest hotel on Market Street. He took another puff on his cigar before telling the concierge to again read the letter that had just been delivered to him from his bank. The man laughed out loud as it was told to him again that all his money from the territorial bank in Santa Fe had been transferred to California. The concierge could not fathom why this was so funny as he left the man sitting there cackling to himself.

After retrieving his bag from the Grand Hotel, Thad met up with Kimberly on the train station platform. She had packed an entire trunk full of her things. "I didn't think you had this much stuff!" he exclaimed. He shook his head as the porter loaded the trunk onto the baggage car. They were taking the evening train south so that they would be in Denver by the following day. After that, a three day trip on the Union Pacific railroad and then the Illinois Central would find them in Chicago by day four.

Thad led her to their seats where he stowed his bag and they waited for the train to depart. Kimberly opened the window and was waving at several friends from Blair Street who had come to see her off. After several minutes, the whistle blew and they were off. Kimberly bounced in her seat with excitement. "I can't wait to see Chicago and all the sights and your family. ..." She leaned over to give him a peck on the cheek. "So, have you told your parents about my past?"

Thaddaeus' eyes grew wide, he hadn't thought of that! *How am I going to tell my mother that I'm marrying a prostitute?*

She giggled and gave him another peck on the cheek, "Well, you'll think of something."

ABOUT JON HOVIS

Jon Hovis is a writer of Western fiction and an associate member of the Western Writers of America, an organization which promotes the literature and authors of the American West. Jon has written two previous books, *The Feather Gang*, and *The Preacher*, both featuring his protagonist Deputy U.S. Marshal Jake Silver. *The Feather Gang* is written as a traditional western story while *The Preacher* and *Silverton Gold* include many historical facts.

Born and raised in Maryland, Jon grew up reading many genres of books including Westerns such as Louis L 'Amour and enjoying Western movies with stars such as John Wayne and Clint Eastwood. After moving to New Mexico as a young man, Jon finds himself living in the west that he used to read about. Jon's books reflect his passion for the history and diversity of the old west. The Southwest is rich in its diverse culture from ancient Indian and pueblo societies to the Spanish and Anglo influences, and a vast range of landscapes from the Rocky Mountains to the high deserts and wild river canyons. Jon's love of this natural beauty inspires his writing and way of life.

Jon currently lives in New Mexico with his wife and daughter. He has played trumpet since his school days and now plays weekly in church and also sings in the choir. His many passions include hiking the American Southwest, exploring remote canyons, mineshafts, ghost towns and Indian ruins, caving and canoeing, and old steam trains.

You can see more information about Jon and his books at his website http://www.jonhovis.com.

Previous releases by Casa de Snapdragon

Arrival
Mary Barnet
Illustrated by
Richard E. Schiff
978-0-9840530-8-7f
Poetry

Storiana
Penelope Weiss
978-0-984053-06-3
Short Stories

Water under Water
Charles Adés Fishman
978-0-9840530-2-5
Poetry

The Making of Tibias Ivory
Through the Eyes of Innocence
D. Allen Jenkins
978-0-9840530-4-9
Relationships, Prejudice

Spectral Freedom
*Select Poetry, Criticism,
and Prose*
Lynn Stongin
Poetry, Short Stories

A Scattering of Imperfections
Katrina K Guarascio
978-0-9793075-8-4
Poetry

Harriet Murphy
A Little Bit of Something
Janet K. Brennan
978-0-9793075-6-0
Short Stories

**I Found My Father in a Women's
Prison**
Tracey Brown, PhD
978-0-9793075-3-9
Christianity, Poetry

Visit us at https://www.casadesnapdragon.com for information on these and other books.

CPSIA information can be obtained at www.ICGtesting.com

229646LV00004B/112/P